Sedona Sunset

Gail Gaymer Martin

ISBN-13: 978-1-947523-43-2
ISBN-10: 1-947523-43-0

Chapter 1

Marcy White's cell phone played its tune as she stood in her bedroom with her Maid of Honor dress halfway over her head. She tugged at the gown, and as it slipped to her shoulders, she grabbed the phone but not recognizing the number, she hit the off button.

She straightened the neckline as she studied herself in the mirror, noting the way the dress draped along her frame. Though she disliked buying clothes, eyeing the gown, her pleasure grew. The bride, Allysa Grant, had selected the dress and pressed her to buy it.

Pressuring her to do anything didn't set well with her. Clamming up had always been her way to deal with that kind of treatment. Even though she resented it at the time, today a sense of gratefulness filled her. "Thanks, Ally. You did a good job." She chuckled hearing her thank you to a friend who wasn't there.

The phone rang again, and she gazed at the number, recognizing it as a local call. She toddled back and forth, but this time, instead of clicking it off, she answered.

"Marcy, this is Grif. Did you hang up on me earlier?"

She squirmed. "Sorry, Grif. I did. My dress and I were in a conflictive situation."

"Ah, then I'm sorry for the interruption. I hope you and the dress are now good friends."

His lighthearted tone caused her to grin. "No need to be sorry. And yes, the dress and I are now companions."

This time he chuckled. "I'll admit I was grateful that Cade didn't want me to wear one of those monkey suits. I already own a suit that I knew would work. I wear it to funerals. You know what I mean? It's dark gray so it's fine for weddings too."

Funerals and weddings. She managed to hold a response while she questioned whether he considered funerals and weddings as equal types of events. "It sounds perfect, Grif." She could picture his broad shoulders filling out a dress suit, though she'd never had the pleasure of seeing him in anything but western attire, much more appropriate for a horse ranch owner.

Grif cleared his throat. "I'm picking you up for the wedding. You know that, right?"

"Ally mentioned it. The wedding's at one o'clock, so when will you be here?"

"I suppose we need to get there early. How about noon or do you think earlier?"

"Maybe eleven thirty, just in case we hit traffic." Being late would never work for Ally. She had a difficult time accepting people's mistakes.

"Okay, eleven-thirty it is." Grif became silent, but she knew he was there. "Can you be ready by then, Marcy?"

She grinned. "I can be. I'll see you then, Grif, and thanks for giving me a ride."

"It's my pleasure. See you soon."

She clicked off the call, understanding his hesitation. Griffin Coleman respected her, even her time. He had a knack for making her smile.

When Marcy eyed the clock, she realized her limited time to get ready. She still had to apply her makeup, along with doing something with her hair, and shoes would be appropriate, too. Her spirit lifted, thinking of Grif in his dark suit and dress shoes.

She shifted to the mirror, cringed at her reflection, then studied her cosmetics. Though limited, she had to do something to make herself look more festive for the wedding. She brushed on a powder foundation, swept a pink blush on her cheeks and colored her lips with a coral-toned lipstick. After scrutinizing her eyes, she grasped the mascara and flicked the brush across her lashes, surprised at how large her eyes became with that added touch.

Her brown eyes almost matched Grif's, except his had flecks of gold, and they looked perfect with his straw-colored hair. Her own drab shade of brown displeased her, although Grif had once mentioned her hair glinted with gold.

Watching the time, she added her earrings and did a last look at herself before slipping on her shoes and hurrying to the living room. When she looked out the window, Grif's car had turned and was rolling up the driveway. She'd just made it.

With autumn in the air, she grasped her beige shawl and tossed it over her arm. Hopefully the warm day would remain through the outdoor wedding. In Marcy's opinion, Ally had been unwise to pick an outside venue, but now that she had chosen that setting, Marcy hoped her day was blessed with good weather.

♥

Grif exited the car just as Marcy stepped outside to the porch. His jaw dropped, seeing how lovely she looked. Marcy always seemed to be a woman who felt no need to gussy up with makeup or fancy clothes. Though she still looked pretty to him, she did little to enhance her natural beauty. He'd admired her when they first met, not so much for her attractiveness, but for her humble demeanor. She spoke softly, offered few opinions and yet listened intently to whatever he rambled about.

When she moved toward the steps, he hurried up the sidewalk to the porch and grasped her hand to guide her down the stairs. He couldn't help but notice as she stepped outside that she'd worn higher heeled shoes than usual, and her lovely coral colored dress puffed outward as it left her waist and widened around her legs. It wasn't a long gown as ones he'd seen at some weddings, but it seemed longer than her usual attire. He feared the skirt would block her next step, and he didn't want to see her trip.

He flinched inside, recognizing his lack of knowledge. He had lots to learn about women if he were to ever pursue a woman to call his own. "You look lovely, Marcy." He hoped that was the right thing to say, since she did look beautiful.

"Thanks, Grif. I'm not used to all this fluff and filmy material. And the shoes? I fear I'll trip and land on my rear."

The image caused him to chuckle, and he hoped it didn't offend her. "I'll stick close so I can catch you before you land on your rump, Marcy."

This time, she tittered at his offer. "Very gallant of you Grif."

He clasped her arm as he guided her around the car to the passenger door and opened it. He stood close by as she slipped onto the seat, and when she'd tucked the dress into the car, he closed the door and hurried around to the driver's side.

Marcy sat in silence until he reached the highway heading for Cade's ranch where the wedding was to take place. Grif opened his mouth a few times to speak and ended up swallowing the words he'd concocted, wanting to have something to say. Too bad they were both quiet.

"You look very handsome, Grif."

His heart skipped when Marcy's soft voice whispered past his ears. "Thank you. As I said, you look very lovely. I realize neither of us are big dresser-uppers."

A hearty guffaw came from her throat, as if she were choking, but instead it turned into a laugh. "Now that's a gem, Grif. Dresser-upper. That's a new one for me."

He grinned. "Glad you like it. I haven't heard it either. I just made it up."

"You're rather creative too. A horseman who is also a language visionary. I'm impressed."

"Don't be." He glanced her way. "I just come up with crazy things that don't make sense to most people. A person has to be special to understand me."

"Then I'm happy to say that I'm special."

His pulse skipped. "You are, Marcy. I noticed that when I met you."

She gave him a questioning look, and he guessed

he'd gone a bit too far. "We're almost there." He figured it was best to change the subject.

Relieved, Grif turned onto Jack's Canyon road and drove up the hill to Lee Mountain where he spotted white helium balloons floating above the gate to Cade's horse ranch, now unlocked and pulled back from the driveway. A few cars were already parked near the house. He heard the wedding would be small, but with both of them active in the community, he suspected many friends would attend.

He pulled through the gate and headed up to the line of cars. After he parked, he perused the situation and noticed that chairs were set up outside, but the barn had been cleaned out and ready for a rain emergency, he suspected. He looked up at the cloudless sky and grinned as he opened Marcy's door. "Perfect weather."

She tilted her head upward and nodded. "I'm glad for them."

He linked his arm to hers and guided her up the dirt driveway toward the white arbor decorated with white flowers and white chairs lined in neat rows, but before he got that far, he heard his name and turned to look behind him. Cade stood in the doorway of the house beckoning them inside.

He faltered. "The groom is signaling us to come in."

Marcy pivoted her head and nodded. "I suppose we'll be told what we have to do as the best man and maid of honor."

He chuckled hearing her say the best man. "At a wedding, wouldn't you think the groom would be the 'best' man?"

She gave him a playful poke. "Then you would be the man of honor."

"True." He gave her arm a pat. As they reached the entrance, he paused and guided Marcy up the one step before joining her at the door.

Cade's voice came from somewhere inviting them inside.

Grif opened the door, motioning Marcy to enter the house, and he followed. Cade appeared around an archway and beckoned them to join him.

"Cade, where's Ally and the girls?" Marcy paused as her gaze swept the living room.

"Come on now, Marcy." He gave her a wink. "You know the rule. The groom can't see the bride before the wedding. My mom and the twins are with Ally at her house. Mom will bring her here when it's time to begin."

"Then maybe I should have asked Grif to stop there, so I could be with the other women."

Cade shook his head. "No, the pastor's in the dining room and wants to go over your responsibilities. You know. It's the typical things you see at every wedding."

Grif gaped at Cade's demeanor, so calm and steady that he couldn't believe his eyes. His own nerves had gotten to him just thinking about the ceremony, and whatever he would have to do. He ignored his unsettled feelings and changed the topic. "You look great, Cade."

"You're not so bad yourself." He gave him a silly grin. "Actually, I've never seen you out of your western getup, I don't think." Cade studied him a moment. "You owe me one, Pal."

Grif scratched his head. "Owe you one what?"

"You owe me for introducing you to the other side of the social world."

Grif gave him a playful punch. "You mean the other

side of the street or the other side of happiness which is misery." He stood back and swept his hand from his shoulder to his toes before tugging on his tie."

Cade only shook his head. "Let me introduce you to Pastor Jack."

He followed Cade into the dining room with Marcy at his side. The pastor, a tall, lean, elderly man, stood near a window that looked out toward the red rocks.

"Pastor Jack, this is my friend Griffin Coleman who will be our best man, and Ally's friend, Marcy White, the maid of honor."

The clergy stuck out his hand and shook hands with him and then Marcy. The pastor then pointed to the chairs. "Let's take a seat, and I can go over this with you. It won't take long."

Grif pulled out a chair for Marcy and then sat beside her, while the pastor sat across from them. Cade had vanished, and Grif assumed that guests were arriving that he wanted to greet. The pastor pointed out their duties. Marcy would hold Ally's bouquet during the vows and make sure her dress and veil were straightened. Grif learned he would help attach their boutonnieres and be responsible for the wedding rings until it was the right time during the ceremony. He pictured his rough fingers trying to hang on to two small rings as he handed them discretely to the bride and groom.

Their responsibilities only took a few minutes, and the pastor rose and slid his chair back under the table. He thanked them, and then walked away while they sat there eyeing each other without speaking.

"I think we can manage everything, don't you?" Marcy flashed him a grin.

He returned a shrug. "I can only see two problems, sticking the boutonniere pin into Cade's chest and dropping the rings with my big ol' hands."

Marcy's brows lifted as she faced him. "What's this big ol' hands comment?" She reached down and lifted his right hand into her palm. "Grif, I like your hands. They are strong and yet gentle, and rugged and yet clean. You're a man who works with horses and mucks stables." Her eyes widened. "Ally told me about that job. Not really 'up my alley' as they say."

Grif chuckled. "Who are the 'theys' everyone talks about?"

"I have no idea, but you get the point."

Again, she made him laugh. Marcy came across as withdrawn and quiet and yet after he got to know her just a little, she surprised him with her soft sense of humor. He liked that about her.

"I get the point and thank you for liking my big ol' hands."

This time she added a playful poke. "I suppose we can go into the living room or even outside to see if we...or I can do anything to help Cade." He eyed his watch. "It's getting close to that time."

Marcy nodded, pushed back the chair and rose before he could assist her. Even though Marcy didn't need his help, he'd directed himself—actually insisted—to continue being chivalrous even if Marcy didn't get what he was doing. He'd never had a lady friend as an adult. As a teen he had female school friends but even then, they did things in groups and never alone which most people referred to as dates.

As they approached the archway, he spotted one of the twins through the living room window. "Ally must be here somewhere. Probably hiding."

"Why do you think that?"

He directed her attention to the window where, now, both twins were evident, each in a pale pink dress and a band in their hair adorned with white flowers. "They look cute, don't you think?"

Marcy didn't respond for a moment, and then he noticed she'd brushed her hands across her eyes. "Marcy, are you cry…ready to go outside?" She would never admit to crying, so why mention it?

She gazed at him, moisture still caught on her lashes. "I'd like to find, Ally."

He hooked his arm through hers. "Let's ask the girls."

As they headed to the door, the reason for Marcy's tears dawned on him. Ally seemed to be her best friend, and after the wedding, Ally would be less available since she would spend most of her time with Cade and the twins. It made sense. His chest tightened thinking of the change for her.

His life would stay pretty much as it had been. The ranch kept him busy, sometimes day and night. Cade had always been a friend, one that shared his passion for horses, and yet not one he hung out with except occasionally. Now that he thought about it, Grif faced the idea that he had always been more of a loner, pretty much like Marcy. They had that in common.

After Marcy talked with the twins, she followed them to Ally's house so she could see her before the wedding, and he returned to the living room, and though bugged by impatience while waiting for something to happen, he remind himself the day belonged to Cade and Ally. It wasn't his day. And never would be.

When the Pastor and Cade appeared, Grif rose and followed them outside as they headed to the arbor and chairs for the guests. As he neared, he eyed white thin fabric draped along the sides of the arbor, decorated with more flowers, mainly white roses but also faint pink flowers of some kind. He stood back, not sure if he should go up front now or wait for Ally. Then he remembered, he and Ally would walk on the white runner leading down the path to the arbor.

The twins hurried beside him, each carrying a basket of flowers plus pink petals which he recalled would be dropped along the white runner. They chattered and giggled, distracting him as only they could do, but their excitement uplifted him. His attitude toward marriage had never been developed.

Marriage had been nowhere in his mind, and he wasn't sure why, but not dating and not seeing a purpose, since his ranch life kept him busy and happy, had to be the obvious reason...until the concept of a legacy had struck a chord in his life, a life that should be more than busy and happy, but one that could be handed down to another generation, life with a purpose.

He lifted his gaze and spotted Marcy heading toward him, her expression purposeful. "It's just about time."

"Now?" He moved closer to her side.

"There's a DJ playing music and when the wedding song begins, we go first, then the twins and then Ally. Cade will be up there already."

He glanced toward the barn and finally saw the DJ's setup and the obvious speakers. As Cade walked to the front, the music began, a song he knew but couldn't remember the name. He hurried to Marcy's side and offered his arm to her. Before they moved forward, he couldn't stop himself. "What's the name of that song?"

She flashed him a grin, not showing a sign of nervousness. "A Thousand Years."

"Right. I suppose that's appropriate for a wedding."

"It is, Grif. The words are beautiful.

He drew back. "You know them."

"Sort of, but I'll tell you later." She tilted her head toward Cade.

He glanced up and noticed Cade gawking at them standing there. "We'd better get moving."

They stepped forward and remembered to walk slowly so Marcy didn't trip on the runner or have a problem with her high heels. When they reached the front, he left Marcy on one side and he shifted beside Cade on the other. As he looked over at Marcy, so striking today, more than he'd ever noticed before, he couldn't believe she knew the words to that song. All he could remember was "for a thousand years."

The prelude grew louder and caught his attention as Chloe and Jolie walked side by side tossing pink petals along the white runner. Behind them, he could see Ally, and to his surprise, Cade's mother Eva walked her down the aisle. Her smile glowed as did Ally's, and it touched his heart.

To him, the unusual combination lifted his spirit. People can make the best of even sad situations. Ally had no contact with her parents and Cade's father had died. But the joy of the wedding radiated all everyone involved. Once in a while, that kind of joy caused him to reconsider his plan to remain single.

The twins stood to the side while the pastor spoke

the wedding vows while Cade and Ally repeated them. Marcy stood close by, holding Ally's white bouquet, and Grif managed to cup the rings in his palm and held them there with his large fingers. He grinned as Marcy's playful comment replayed in his mind. She said she liked his "big ol' hands." But then, kindness seemed to live inside Marcy.

When it came time to give Cade the rings, he managed it without dropping them as relief swept through him. The rest of his duties left him no concern. He watched the rings slide on their fingers and then the pastor's announcement caused everyone to smile. "You are now Mr. and Mrs. Cade Murphy, followed by the words everyone waited for. "You may now kiss the bride."

The sweet kiss caused Grif's heart to skip. Had he ever kissed a woman not counting his mother. He couldn't recall so if he had it had made no impression. His romantic life could be etched on the end of the nail on a horse hoof. Pitiful.

The bride and groom headed down the aisle followed by the twins. He and Marcy ended the procession as the guests gathered behind them to congratulate Ally and Cade. When he reached them, the twins nestled beside them, excitement sparkling in their eyes. Chloe leaned toward them. "Ally's my new mommy."

"She's my mommy, too." Jolie's expression had added a spark of irritation at her sister.

"You both have a new mommy, girls." Marcy gave each a pat. "You are very blessed."

Both gave a huge nod. "We're blessed."

Grif squeezed Marcy's arm. "Good job."

As they stepped back, Marcy glanced at him with a grin. "I'm trying to learn about children."

He longed to ask her why, but then it wasn't his business. Still, the interest made him curious, knowing her stand on romance. His pulse jigged thinking perhaps her attitude had changed after seeing the joy the twins gave to Ally. He'd heard Ally's goal focused on fun and adventure and look at her now.

He managed to cover his grin as if being cordial to the guests who were standing in line around the bride and groom. Yes, he'd changed, too. No question. New interests and ideas slipped into his mind before he realized where they had come from. They'd settled in his mind as concern for having a legacy. Leaving his ranch and any good things he'd done to someone in his family. He had none. His parents were gone. He had no siblings. He was his family.

The DJ had changed the tone of the music and now country music and some popular tunes about love billowed across the grass enticing the guests and the wedding party to enter the barn where the meal and celebration would continue.

When he tucked away his thoughts and focused, Marcy stood nearby gazing at him as if trying to decide if he'd gone into a trance or had died standing up. His silly thought caused him to grin, but she could be correct. He'd paused too long while staring into space, and he had things to do to help Cade get everyone inside.

"We have a job, I guess." He answered Marcy's question without her asking. He tucked her arm beneath his, and they headed toward the barn, decorated on the outside with white and pink streamers and a sign that said, "Let's Celebrate."

"We're not the first ones." Marcy tilted her head toward a few people already seated at the long tables.

Grif recalled Cade had rented all the equipment. The tables were covered with white cloths and decorated with a bouquet of white and pink flowers. "Amazing what a person can do with a barn."

"It is." Marcy scanned the barn nearly in full circle. "I recall seeing all kinds of things in here including bales of hay. I wonder what—"

"If this were my party, I'd store them in the stable, at least temporarily." Marcy's inexperience with farm life tickled him. "Didn't Ally tell you what they'd planned."

"You know, Ally. She didn't say much. I think she wanted to surprise everyone, and you know how people are. If you tell them what you're doing, at least half of them will have a better idea or warn you of every possible problem."

"That could be." Her attitude surprised him…or did it? Marcy kept her opinions to herself so often. He longed at times to probe her thoughts that he recognized on her face, but attitudes that weren't spoken. Such a wonderful woman, and yet closed up like a box. Why?

Instead of prodding her for reasons or answers, he kept quiet. He wanted to enjoy the day, and even more, he wanted Marcy to enjoy the day.

Hearing more voices, he turned his attention to the wide barn doorway and watched many people amble into the barn, gaze around, as he and Marcy had, admiring all the work they'd accomplished to make it a festive and good-looking setting for a wedding reception.

Marcy gave a wave, and Grif eyed the woman, assuming she worked at the hospital. He'd never seen her locally.

When Marcy wandered off, a sense of loneliness surrounded him. The sensation surprised him more than he could have ever imagined. He'd always been alone, and it never bothered him any more than the shake of a horse's tail, but today he found himself lost.

Reviewing his job to encourage people inside, he took a step and then stopped as Marcy approached him. "Grif, I want you to meet one of my coworkers. This is Kelly Redmond. She works in the Step-down Unit where I usually am. It's either Step-down or 'the Floor.'"

Floor? That was new to him.

Marcy chuckled. "That's a place where patients who are there for a few tests or need IV medication or specific treatments, but otherwise, can do most everything for themselves."

He chuckled. "Sort of a 'catch-all,' it sounds like."

Kelly grinned. "You could say that."

"Nice to meet you, Kelly." He extended his hand, and she gave it a firm shake, and then looked across the room.

"I see some friends from work over there. I supposed I should get a seat before they're gone."

Marcy nodded and turned to him. "I'm going over to stay hello, and then I think we're supposed to encourage people to eat the hors d'oeuvres. Is that right?"

"You're right. I forgot." He took a step toward the table and then paused. "Go ahead and say hello to your friends, and I'll start with some of the filled tables.

People will catch on."

"Thanks, Grif." She turned away and crossed the room.

Once he reached the spread of appetizers, Grif tried a couple and then looked around to see if anyone had begun. He saw one table with a few appetizers on a plate, so he moved on to the next table. As people rose to try the treats, the DJ played an unexpected fanfare as Cade and Ally stepped through the wide doorway.

People stood and applauded, and as they moved in, stopping at tables as they worked their way toward the head table, numerous guests finally rose and made their way to the first course. This best man job was new to him, and he wished he could have been a guest and just enjoy the day. But Cade had asked, and he had done what was right.

His spirit lifted when Marcy headed his way and beckoned him to follow her. He anticipated meeting new friends, but in a flash, he realized, they were to be seated at the head table. Instead of going directly there, he grasped a plate and tried a few of the appetizers displayed for the guests.

Marcy shook her head with a smile, but joined him. "We might as well." Though more selective, she filled her plate also, and they joined Cade and Ally. As he sat, his nerves zipped up his limbs. He'd forgotten until that moment that he had to do a toast. He'd prepared nothing.

Chapter 2

Marcy settled beside Grif at the table, and yet Grif seemed far from settled. His leg bounced beside her bumping the skirt of her fluffy gown. She longed to ask him what was wrong, but then she could almost guess. He was sorry he had to be burdened with her for the whole day.

Her head drooped as the words ran through her mind. Why did she say that? The old Marcy had crept out of the trunk again. How long did it take to let go of the past and look for a brighter future? She didn't enjoy being with people who were glum and pitiful. And that's not who she wanted to be.

"You're quiet."

She jumped, hearing Grif's comment. "Edgy, I guess. Being part of a wedding is new to me."

"Me, too. I'm great on the ranch. I know my job and the horses are like friends. I've had nice conversations with you, Marcy, but I'm not a social bug…or whatever they call it."

Unable to control her chuckle, she let it go. "I believe that's called a social butterfly."

"Ah." He tilted his head and grinned. "I'm not even social enough to know that."

"Oh, Grif, I'm so unsocial, I'm surprised I knew what you meant."

He slipped his arm around the back of her chair. "I think we make a good team, Marcy. What could be better?"

She couldn't answer the question, because she had no answer. Instead, she managed to smile.

As the room quieted, Grif's knee bounced even more as he leaned closer. "Oh-oh, it's time for me to say something, and I didn't give it a smidgeon of thought. He pushed back his chair, gave her one of his "here-goes" looks and rose. "Welcome everyone. Tonight, we're here to celebrate the wedding of our friends, Ally and Cade. Being a long-time friend, I was around to watch their relationship begin as they bumped into few red rocks and yet cantered through the meadow with smiles on their faces. I'm really happy to see this here cowboy…" He flicked his thumb toward Cade. "…fall in love with this very pretty cowgirl. And I think Chloe and Jolie are happy, too."

He grinned as they girls jumped up and clapped their hands giving Ally a hug. "Let's raise our glasses and wish these two many, many years of what they call 'wedded bliss.' I think that's what they call it." The guests broke into a rousing laugh.

As the noise died down, he raised the stemmed goblet. "Lord, bless Ally and Cade with a lifetime of happiness and joy, and if times gets rough, stand beside them and guide them through the darkness back into the light of love and commitment."

He turned to face them. "Ally and Cade, I am honored to be here to share in the celebration of your lives together—all four of you."

Cade and Ally had risen and they lifted their glasses. Cade nodded. "Amen, Grif, and thanks to all of you who are here today."

Applause followed, but before he could set down, Maggie tugged his arm. "Bless the food, so we can eat."

This time he chuckled. "We don't want to miss that." He set down the goblet and quieted the group. "Before we enjoy the meal, let's bow our head. Dear Lord, we thank you for this food, for those who prepared it, and for those who are here to celebrate with two people who have found their soul mates, Ally and Cade. Bless this food to our bodies and bless Ally and Cade's steps into their marriage. Amen."

"Amen" echoed against the barn's high ceiling, and this time Grif settled into his chair, his neck and back tense, hoping what he said made sense.

Marcy lifted her hand and rested in on his. "You were joking about not being prepared, weren't you?"

A frown tugged at his face until he managed to overcome his surprise. "No. Not at all. That was off the cuff."

"You have an amazing cuff, Grif. What you said was beautiful and appropriate. I'm really proud of you. I couldn't have done that."

"Sure, you could."

She shook her head veraciously. "I would have bumbled and stumbled trying to put words together that made sense. I don't talk to people. You know the old saying,'Be seen and not heard."

Pressure filled her chest speaking those words. She never wanted to hear them again. She'd lived with those five words ringing in her ears day and night.

"Not you, Marcy. You should be seen and heard.

I'm not sure where you learned that old saying, but it doesn't fit you at all." He slipped her hand into his and gave it a squeeze."

The pressure in her chest grew, but this time for a different reason.

Grif rose with her hand still in his and tilted his head toward the buffet table. "Did they tell us to—"

"We're at the head table, remember. The bride and groom always start the meal."

She nodded, but a shrug would have been more truthful. Weddings had been few in her family, and if she'd attended, the memory had been lost somewhere in her head.

She walked beside Grif, with the twins in front of them. To assist Ally, she would see if she could help the girls plate their meals. Eyeing the table, she admired the attractive presentation of the food. The hors d'œuvre where gone and in their place, were large chafing dishes with meats and vegetables, huge glass bowls filled with salad greens and diced vegetables, baskets filled with bread and dinner rolls, and a variety of relishes— pickles, ripe and green olives and small peppers.

To her surprise, Grif asked Chloe if he could help her with her plate. She grinned and let him dish up the food as she held the plate. The same worked with Jolie when she asked. The task went fast and without any problems. Ally grinned and mouthed thank you to them when she saw what they had done.

Marcy selected a chicken drumstick, a slice of tender beef, cheese potato casserole, and a helping of vegetables along with a salad. Though her plate looked filled, she stopped herself from laughing when seeing Grif's high mounded plate filled with his choices. He grinned at her and whispered in her ear. "I'm still growing."

He looked like a little boy trying to sweet-talk his mom. She'd never been fascinated by a man in her life, but Grif had the knack. "I hope growing up and not growing out."

He gave her a wink as they headed back to their table, while the line grew as the guests headed toward the buffet, table by table.

As the room quieted, the DJ selected soft background dinner music—instrumental versions of old classics, love songs and sweet melodies she didn't recognize, but the tender tunes that seemed appropriate. She nibbled at the delicious food, her stomach still tight from emotions that grasped her when she least expected it.

Desserts filled a table, the lovely wedding cake, decorated differently with its bride and groom on horseback, and trays of cookies and dessert bars with coffee and tea urns nearby. "I'll wait on desserts, Grif, so if you'd like to—"

"I'd like to sit here with you. You're sweet enough." He touched her hand again, sending a sizzling sensation up her arm. He'd startled her with his comment, and all she could do was say thank you. She longed to say more but couldn't.

"By the way…" He leaned closer, curiosity written on his face. "Tell me about that song they used for the bride's walk down the aisle. A million years…or something like that."

She pressed her lips together to keep from laughing. "A thousand years, but it could be a million, too, I suppose."

"Right. A thousand years. You said you'd tell me about the song."

"It's nothing that dramatic, really, but it's appropriate for a wedding, especially people who struggled with their own self-doubt and longings, and yet they're afraid to comment." Her heart trembled against her breast bone as she realized the words captured her own feelings when she considered love or wanted it...and yet...

"That sort of sounds like me, Marcy. Love is something I've feared to give, but I've learned that we don't always have control. It happens and then we ask ourselves what if and will she...or in your case, will he return the love." He lowered his head in silence before inching his chin upward. "Do you know what I mean?"

"I do, Grif. I do." She dug into her mind for the words. "It talks about having loved someone like the person she is with, breath freezing when they first met, questioning, and yet it ends with a beautiful promise. That he'd loved her for a thousand years, and he'll love her for a thousand more."

Grif stared into space, and she feared he might laugh or walk away. Instead, he turned to her and gave a faint nod. "Sometimes it takes a lot of thought to find the answer to something important. I've made business decisions with that same kind of stress, but that's different from relationships—not just friendships, but ones with commitments of forever love."

"That can be scary, can't it?" When she saw his expression, she wished she'd kept her mouth shut, but his surprise melted into a grin. "A life commitment can be scary, and yet people do it all the time. We just watched Ally and Cade say the words, 'until death parts us.' That's a huge commitment."

"Do you believe it, Grif?"

"You know what, Marcy. I do. I think that there is real love, love that works its way into a person's heart and soul. The soul is important. When that happens, I think a man and woman can say those words. Until death parts us."

Her pulse skipped along her arms, as she watched a kind of joy fill his face. "I agree, Grif. My parents had an odd marriage. My dad was the king of the house, and what he said was as if God had spoken. My mom was a woman who could remain quiet, do what she had to do, and sometimes do what she wanted without letting him know. They managed, but it wasn't what I wanted, and staying single seemed the best for me, rather than take a chance."

"Do you feel the same now?"

His gaze probed hers, and her breath seeped from her lungs. Avoiding a gasp, she gathered her wits and her response. "Not anymore, Grif. I am cautious, but in the past years, I've seen marriages that were blessed with the kind of love that I think marriage should mean. I'm more open to the possibility, but..."

His eyes widened when she remained silent. She hadn't meant to confuse him, but she had confused herself. But what? The word popped out of her mouth and she had no idea what words should follow.

He gazed at her while she fought her desire to shrink into the chair cushion. "Sorry, I didn't mean to upset you."

"You didn't upset me, Marcy. You made me curious."

"It did the same to me." She grinned.

Grif broke out in a laugh as she shook his head. "That's good. We can work on that together." He pointed to the dance floor. "Cade and Ally just walked to the dance floor. I think we're to follow them shortly."

Dance. She hadn't danced in decades. Maybe never, except in her exercise class when they did movements that the leader said was like the Charleston or the two-step. Her pulse charged and her heartbeat joined the rhythm. But how could she say no?

She turned to watch Cade and Ally move around the floor, swaying and twirling, and when she noticed Cade beckoning Grif, blood drained from her veins.

"It's our turn." He rose and reached out for her hand.

As if glued to the chair, she stared up at him, thinking her legs wouldn't hold her. "Grif, I don't really—"

"I don't either, but we can move to the rhythm. Let's do our best."

She couldn't argue with his commonsense, so she rose and let him steer her onto the dance floor. All eyes were on them, it seemed, and yet most were looking at Ally and Cade, so why worry?

Grif slipped his arm around her back and drew her closer while his free hand grasped hers and held it against his chest. He swayed to the love song, shifting his feet to the right and then to the left, and after she'd caught on, he twirled her around. Though uncomfortable, she managed to end up back in his arms, and his smile sent her soaring.

"You're a good dancer, Marcy." He held her close, his feet sweeping to the right and the left, yet she managed to follow, loving the feel of his arms around her, his smile warming her heart.

The music came to an end, and people applauded as the bride and groom left the floor, and Cade returned with his mom. Grif didn't move but stood with her still in his arms, and when the next song began, Marcy's heart swelled. "I love this song."

The music began, and as *All of Me* wove through her heart, she closed her eyes, amazed that Grif was singing the words in a whisper with the wonderful sound of John Legend. Unable to speak, she listened until the song ended, and she stood in his arms, gaping at him. "Grif, you have a really nice voice."

"Not usually. I just happen to like that song too."

His excuse fell flat, but she added it to his humble demeanor. Grif would never admit that he had a talent outside the realm of being a horse rancher.

The next piece, though another love song, picked up the beat, and she eased her steps toward their table, not wanting to embarrass herself. But as she neared the table, she noticed Jolie and Chloe with longing looks at the dance floor and bouncing up and down. How could she ignore them?

She stood close and beckoned them to her. Smiles bloomed on their faces like sunflowers, and they dashed to her side, their pretty pink dresses bouncing as they ran. "Do you like this song?"

They nodded, and as she stepped toward the dance floor, Grif joined her and they got into a circle with a girl between them and bounced around to the song, *Marry You*. Even though she couldn't dance, she recalled some of her exercise steps and decided to have fun.

Ally and Cade swung by, smiles on their faces, and waved to the girls. The twins glowed as they bounced along with them keeping the beat as good as she had.

If her arm was long enough, she might pat herself on the back for being thoughtful and even more for tossing out her pride to let the girls have fun. And Grif too. He appeared to be enjoying himself as much as the girls.

When the song ended, they stood gasping, and though Marcy didn't like sending the girls back, she and Grif needed a break. Before they moved a foot, the plan altered in a good way. Ally and Cade joined them and led the twins onto the dance floor. The music had slowed again, and they took turns with each girl, dancing with their daddy and another turn with their new step-mom.

Grif steered her to the dessert table, and though she still had little room for food, she eyed the desserts and couldn't resist. They headed back to the table with a sample of a few of the delicious looking bars and a small piece of wedding cake.

They sat in silence nibbling on the desserts and drinking the coffee that Grif had gone back to bring them. He finished first and gazed at her, making her uncomfortable, although his expression was a grin. "What are you thinking?"

He shook his head. "Nosey, aren't you?"

"No, Curious."

"Is that what they call it?" He grasped her hand. "You surprise me, Marcy. You have more talents than you're willing to admit, and I wish I knew why."

She shrugged. "I don't think I'm talented, really.

I'm an okay nurse practitioner. I do my job well. I'm a faithful friend, but other than that…" She shrugged again.

"You can dance. You can't deny that."

She laughed, facing the reason why she could. "I used the moves from an exercise class I took once."

"But you did well, and you have rhythm."

"And you can sing, Grif. Who would know that?"

He raised his hand and brushed his finger along her cheek. "I might have talents you can't even imagine, Marcy."

"Now I'm curious."

"I can rope a calf. Never tried a bull, but I might be able to do that, and I'm pretty good on a horse."

"You see…I can't do any of those things."

"But you could. I'll teach you."

"Me?" Her pitch raised to the sky. "Oh no, you're starting to sound like Ally. She wanted me to go on a hot air balloon ride. She wanted me to take riding lessons with her. She's wanted me to do all kinds of crazy things. I won't do them."

"Why?"

"Because."

Grif slipped his arm around her again. "That's not an answer. It's a cop-out. Give me a reason."

♥

Marcy had never been belligerent in front of Grif, but now was the time. He didn't need to know why, and actually she didn't know either. Fear, maybe. She'd grown up with her father bellowing in her face that women were meant to do housework and raise children. Nothing more. She stared at Grif without a word.

He lowered his head. "Sorry. I guess it's not my

business why you shortchange your life." He drew in a ragged breath, staring into space for a few moments. "Really, Marcy. I'll shut up. It was wrong to bug you."

The more she thought about it, the more she realized he was right. "Forgive me, Grif. Maybe someday I can talk about it. But not now."

He nodded, and she ached seeing his sad eyes, so heartbreaking she feared she might cry. The DJ had taken a break, and unable to control her fluctuating emotions, she turned her attention across the room to Ally and Cade visiting the guests at the tables. Though Ally glowed, Marcy suspected that something was wrong. She knew Ally well enough to read her expressions, and Marcy's chest constricted.

Not wanting to say anything to Grif, she waited, hoping that she would have an opportunity to talk with them. The music began again, but instead of dancing, Cade led Ally back toward the head table.

Marcy swallowed her confusion as she dug into her thoughts to decide how to ask the sensitive question. Having second thoughts, she studied Grif's face and his look answered her question. "You're concerned about something, aren't you?"

He gave a one-shoulder shrug and then nodded. "I'm wondering—"

"What's going on with Ally and Cade. Am I right?"

His neck tilted back, a surprised look washing over him as he searched her face. "You see something too?"

"I do. And Grif, I'm positive it isn't reflecting their marriage or anything like that. It's something else."

"Yep, that's what I'm thinking. But what?"

This time a ragged breath slipped past her throat. "I can only guess and I'm sure I'd be wrong. I noticed his mother left, and I wonder if they had an argument or something, but it's not like his mother. She's one of the sweetest people there is, according to Ally."

"She is. I've known her for years. I wonder if she's ill or …" His brow wrinkled. "That would cause both of them to be worried and distracted."

"True. They're heading this way. Should we ask?"

"Give them a minute to tell us first."

Her pulse skipped. Grif always seemed to know the right thing to do. "Right."

They sat on the edge of their chairs, and when Ally slipped onto the chair and Cade joined her, they sat in silence. Not one word. Marcy glanced at Grif, but he gave a faint shake of his head. She closed her mouth.

Cade finally looked at them. "It's been an amazing day, but I supposed you can tell we have a problem."

They both remained silent and gave a nod. A few moments passed before Grif spoke first. "Is there anything we can do to help?"

Cade shook his head. "Not really, Grif, but thanks. My mom started getting ill earlier today but you know her, she put on her I'm-just-fine act. But she couldn't handle it the whole night. She finally admitted she wasn't well and thought she should go home."

Ally slipped her arm around his shoulders. "An old friend of Cade's had to leave early, and he volunteered to take her home, but we fear she might need to go to the hospital or something, so we want to go to see her after we leave tonight, and if we wait until the end, that could be late."

Marcy shook her head. "It's your wedding, Ally. The bride and groom often leave early to catch a plane or whatever for the honeymoon."

Cade lowered his head. "And that's our other problem. We have reservations, but I can't leave my mom alone and naturally, she was the one who had volunteered to take care of the girls the week we're gone."

Marcy's heart sank. They faced a nearly hopeless situation, and neither she nor Grif could solve that many problems. "Why don't you make an announcement that you're leaving and whatever else you need to say. Leave the girls with us, and if you leave the door unlocked, we'll get them into the house and stay with them until you take care of your mom, Cade. Then we can see what has to happen next."

Cade shook his head. "I can't do that to you two. You're the greatest friends but it's too much—"

Grif raised off the chair and leaned closer to Cade. "You just said it, Cade. We're the greatest friends. What do friends do for each other? We don't walk away when there's a problem. We stand by each other. We'll do exactly what Marcy said."

Ally's glazed eyes lost their battle and tears rolled down her cheeks. Marcy reached out and took Ally's hand. "Please leave. You can be honest and tell your friends that you're concerned about Eva, and we'll take care of the girls. They'll be worried so we'll go inside shortly. It'll give you time to see what's going on with your mom, Cade."

Ally and Cade eyed each other and finally Ally nodded. "We can't thank you enough. You two are the best friends anyone could want."

Grif chuckled. "Then get out of here before we change our minds."

They held hands, walked across the room, stopping

to talk with the twins, and then over to the DJ. They made the announcement, followed by the guests verbal concern and sadness as well as their well-wishes. With a wave, Cade and Ally made their way to the door, and as they stepped out, Chloe and Jolie hurried to her and Grif asking a million questions—it seemed like a million since they both talked at the same time.

♥

Grif had the girls sit between him and Marcy so they could explain and soothe their fears. He had no idea how serious Cade's mother was, but he prayed she had a flu bug or something that could be treated without any major steps, such as hospitalization. When the twins settled down, Marcy suggested they see if the caterer had a box so they could take a few more desserts home. She gave him a subtle wink which let him know her hope was that it would distract them and give them something to look forward to. Marcy went with them, and soon they were back with a box filled with sweet treats.

He noticed the girls were antsy, and rather than sit there with all four of them miserable and worried, they rose and stopped on their way to the barn door to speak with a friend or two and explain their departure. The girls followed without complaint.

In the dim light from the moon, they headed toward the house. Cade left the porch light on, and she saw he'd also left a light on in the living room. Marcy took over going with the girls to their bedroom, and he was grateful that she hadn't wanted him to give a pep talk before they were sent to bed. His pep had drained to nothing.

He could hear Marcy's voice floating in the room,

but it was only a soft buzz so he had no idea what she was saying, but he knew she would be wonderful with the girls. Marcy had a knack that she didn't realize, and he hoped one day, she would realize the gifts she'd been given as she dealt with people. She used the skills on her job, and it was natural to carry over into her life. Or more likely, it was the other way around.

He sat racking his brain for what to do next. Though he wanted to call Cade, he hesitated. He might be in the hospital or talking with a doctor or... Too many unknowns piled in front of him like a bulwark. He rarely felt helpless, but he did at the moment.

The voices quieted, and he gazed at the doorway, waiting to see Marcy come through the door. He stared like a watchman with only the silence accompanying him. After a few minutes, he heard a noise, footsteps, and Marcy entered the room, shaking her head. His spirit sank. "What's wrong?"

"Ally called me. She said Cade would call you shortly."

"What's going on?"

"Apparently Eva has a bad virus of some kind, and of all things, it turned into pneumonia. She's in the hospital." She blew out a stream of air. "They're saying goodbye to their honeymoon, and that breaks my heart."

"Believe it or not, it makes me sad, too. They deserve a honeymoon, but I understand why they can't go."

"Apparently the doctor told them, she will be alright, but they're keeping her hospitalized because of her age and also to make certain that it doesn't get worse so she would need extra treatment. The doctor told them to go. But—"

"But they won't." He rolled his eyes, and yet he understood. "Marcy, what can we do to help?"

"I don't know, Grif. His mother is going to be at Verde Valley Medical Center. I'm there so I could stop by and visit with her, and report in to Cade. They could call and check every day. The nurses are great about that, and they understand. We do that all the time for people who are concerned."

"Then why don't they go ahead. Wait a day maybe and then head out."

"The girls. That's the big problem."

He dropped back against the chair cushion. "Right. How could I forget that? It's a big problem, but there must be a solution somehow."

"I can be with the girls after work. I could spend the evening with them and sleep here at night. But I work, so I'd have to do something about that. I can see if I could get some time off, but—"

"Okay, listen. You can be here after work and through the night. You work in Cottonwood so you can bring the girls to the ranch and they can spend the day with me. I can keep them busy and then you can pick them up at night. What do you think?"

Marcy stared at the floor, her lips pressed together as if keeping herself from saying something she didn't want to say.

He leaned forward, sorting through the details. He couldn't understand why it wouldn't work. He had the horses. The girls would love helping him feed the horses. He could have them clean the stable with him, maybe not muck it out, but do other things. They were seven-years-old and they already lived on a horse ranch.

"Grif, that could work if you think you could handle it. I'm willing to do it for Ally. She's been a dear friend for a long time. She puts up with my oddities and other than trying to pry me out of my box, which she thinks is a good thing, we get along great. Her friendship means a lot to me."

"I can do it, Marcy. I'm not concerned at all. I think the girls will enjoy their time here. They live on a ranch so it will be almost like home to them."

"You're right. I can call Ally and tell her or...maybe—"

"I'll call Cade. I know that's what you want and since they are his daughters, he might accept the plan knowing I'm all for it. Maybe one day, he can do the same for me."

Marcy grinned. "You mean take care of your daughters?"

He chuckled and shook his head. "Not quite, but do me a big favor. You never know."

"I agree. Cade might be more likely to listen to you than me."

"Don't think he doesn't like you. I—"

"I didn't mean that. She sank to the arm of his chair and rested her hand on his shoulder. "I mean that women are often more willing to babysit than men, I think. If he knew you were willing and had no worries about it, he might say yes. I want them to have a nice time getting away for a few days."

"So do I. So, let me call, and we'll see what happens.

Chapter 3

Grif headed home while Marcy stretched out on the couch with a blanket and pillow she found in the linen closet. Not knowing when they would show up, or who else might arrive, she tossed and turned for at least an hour before drifting off to sleep.

Noise awakened her, and she jerked up from the pillow as Ally followed by Cade stepped into the living room. "How are things with your mother, Cade?"

"She's going to be fine. I believe them. They've been great to us with all the waiting and worrying."

"Good news, Ally. And I agree since we both know from working there that it is a good hospital." She longed to ask their plans, but she kept her mouth closed which was rare for her. Ally could validate that.

Ally pressed her hand to her heart and closed the distance between them as she plopped on the edge of the couch beside her. "I'm sorry that you had to stay so long, Marcy. You're going to be exhausted tomorrow, and I know you have work."

"Actually, I don't. I traded off with someone knowing that I might be up late at the wedding so I figured not having to go in would be a treat."

"That makes me feel better." Ally rested her hand

on Marcy's arm and gave it a pat. "Thanks so much. You and Grif were life savers. We both were worried, and it was difficult trying to be at the reception when our minds were with Eva."

"I know. I can read your expression fairly well after all these years being friends. I knew you were upset, and I knew that you both belonged with Eva to see what was wrong."

Cade moved closer. "You and Grif are the dearest friends we have, Marcy. And I mean that."

"Thanks, Cade." She opened her mouth and then closed it. "You're telling me the doctors say you have no worries."

He nodded. "We can't help but be concerned and yet they insisted we go on our honeymoon, but we—"

"But you thought you had no one to be with the girls."

A frown settled on Cade's face. "What do you mean we thought?"

Marcy drew back. "Didn't Grif call you?"

He glanced at Ally and stood a moment before he dug into his pocket and pulled out his phone. "I forgot the call. The call came when we were talking to the doctors. I felt the phone vibrate. I had the ring tone turned off."

Marcy's heart sank. She'd hoped that Grif had handled it, and now it had been left to her.

"Okay, wait." Cade hit some buttons, and Grif's voice came from the phone, explaining their plan. Cade grinned. "As you hear, he left a voice mail."

"I'm glad he called you. He said he would."

"Sorry, I missed it." He glanced at Ally and then turned to Marcy. "Listen, we can't do that to you and

Grif. That's a big responsibility and—"

"And you think that your two dear friends are too inept to take care of the girls for a few days. We worked it out with no problem. I'll spend the evening and night with them here at your house and take them to Grif's in the morning on my way to work, and they'll enjoy being at a home away from home. They know ranch life, and they know Grif and me. Why wouldn't that work?"

Cade's jaw dropped and he turned to Ally. "Why wouldn't it?"

Ally broke into a laugh. "It would work, Cade. Our friends want to help us. Will you accept? I think the girls will love it. It's like they're on a honeymoon too."

"It is?" He eyed Ally a moment and then laughed. "I suppose it's different, at least."

Marcy pointed toward the doorway. "Alright, it's settled. Now get yourself ready and be on your way. You're going to California, right?"

Cade nodded. "It's not too far, and we're staying at a resort on the ocean. Something different for two people who live on the desert."

"I'd say so." Marcy patted Cade's back. "It'll be wonderful. You can Facetime the girls, or maybe you have Duo. Whichever. We can work it out even if you just call to talk with them."

Ally shifted her focus to Marcy. "Are the girls sleeping?"

"They are, and no problem. They were tired and didn't squawk."

Cade gave her a thumbs up. "Good for you, Marcy. I might hire you to be our nanny."

"And I might enjoy it, Cade."

Ally's eyes widened. "Goodness, what's happening to my long-time friend who never wanted to deal with children…or marriage for that matter."

"I still don't know about marriage, but kids aren't so bad."

Everyone laughed at that, except when she pictured what Grif's expression might be, she cringed. "I gave kids a chance so I might learn that marriage is amazing. Who knows?"

She'd hoped to lighten the moment, and yet her chest ached knowing she'd somehow hurt Grif and yet not sure why.

♥

Grif tried to ignore Marcy's comment about not wanting to deal with marriage, but he couldn't and wrestled during the night, getting little sleep as her attitude hit him in the face. He knew she had reservations about most everything she'd never experienced. She doubted herself, and he wished he understood why.

But that wasn't his problem today. Today, he teetered on the answer to the questions swinging in his head like a pendulum. Did Marcy care about him? He'd become confident that they did have something special happening. Even with her limited ability to express her feelings, he could see reactions and emotion in her face. But his judgment faded. Maybe he didn't know her at all.

Longing to find the answers, his growing question remained on the teeter-totter in his head. He could do more harm than good. Though she would drop by soon with the girls, they had no alone time to talk, and getting away from the twins would be impossible…unless he could be creative. No, it was impossible.

Marcy had taken off yesterday, so she could spend the full day with the girls while he rattled around trying to handle his confusion, but today the agreed-upon plan for the girls' care began.

He sat in his recliner sipping his hot coffee. Breakfast had limped from his mind which was too full of everything but food. As he stared into space, he heard a noise outside. His chest knotted with a tangle of concern, worry, curiosity and a smidgeon of hope.

As the girls' piping voices grew closer, he set down his coffee and pushed himself from the chair, hoping he could look normal when he answered the door. When he pulled it open, Marcy's eyes searched his.

"We're here. Two eager young ladies and me." She gave him a strained smile.

"Come in." He stepped back and pushed the door open wider. "Did the girls get breakfast?"

"We had cereal and—"

"Fruit and Marcy gave us a healthy cookie." Chloe ended Jolie's response.

Grif couldn't help but chuckle. "A healthy cookie? Hmm? Now what could that be?"

Marcy grinned. "Oatmeal cookies with raisins. I hope you like raisins because I brought you a dozen or so. I made them a few days ago and froze them." She handed him the paper bag. "They're thawed now."

Her lighthearted conversation and the gift added a measure of growth to his hope. "I love oatmeal and raisins are great. When I was a kid, I called them rotten grapes, but then I learned the truth."

"Yuk. Rotten grapes." Chloe curled up her nose.

"They're not rotten. We learned how grapes turn into raisins."

"They're dried." Jolie elbowed her way into the conversation. "That's how they become raisins."

Grif rested a hand on each girl. "And did you know that plums turn into prunes when they're dried."

"Really?" Chloe's eyes widened.

Jolie folded her arms. "Can people dry apples and oranges and—"

Marcy gave him a helpless grin. "Girls, many things can be dried and yes apples can be dried, and they're sold as dried apples, but not everything can be dried. It's good that we can dry plums and grapes."

Jolie gave a big nod. "We can use them to make healthy cookies."

Grif slipped his arm around both the girls' shoulders. "Right. Healthy cookies are important." He dropped his hands from their shoulders. "Now, Marcy needs to go to work, so we need to say goodbye so she's not late.

Marcy nodded. "By the way, I tossed a couple of other things into that sack. I nearly forgot to tell you." She lowered her gaze to the girls. "I'll be back around five-thirty or so...maybe six, so be ready to leave okay, girls?" She took another step but then paused again.

Both girls nodded, their voices echoing they would be ready, and she moved forward again and approached the door.

Grif followed hoping to get a minute to say something...anything to help him relax. Before he could reach her, the twins had tagged along, too, so all he could do was to let her know he'd see her later.

He watched her pull away while the girls appeared

to have vanished. When he turned around, he suspected they were touring the house. Their voices rose and fell as they spotted things that seemed to catch their interest.

When he found them, they were in the kitchen looking in the cabinets. They spun around when they heard him, and Jolie rushed forward. "We're looking for oatmeal, so we can bake some—"

"Bake?" A chill ran down his back. "Marcy brought us a dozen cookies, and I think you've probably had enough cookies for now. Let's do something else. What do you say?"

Though their expression pinched, they stared at him as if waiting for the verdict. "Would you like to help me with the horses? We need to put them into the corral for exercise, and I'm sure I have some carrots and apples—not dried ones—for their treat."

Their eyes widened and they both bounded forward.

"Let's go." Chloe was the first to dart toward the kitchen door.

"Hang on Chloe. We can go this way." He pointed to the back door. "It's closer and the treats are in a shed nearby."

They spun in that direction and flung open the door. Before he could gather his wits, they were charging toward the shed that stood close to the stables. As he walked, it dawned on him that he'd committed to these young ladies for a week or so, and he'd given his assistant Buck a week off that he'd asked for. What had he been thinking?

But when he met up with the girls at the shed door, their faces glowed with excitement and a kind of innocence. They must have helped Cade with the horses, but his horses were new and exciting to them, he guessed. "Okay, let's grab some apples."

Each girl picked up what they could hold and hugged them to their chests as they followed him toward the stable. As they moved closer, he heard a faint whinny and guessed one of the horses was feeling neglected. The thought made him grin.

"I heard a horse. Did you?" Jolie looked up into his face.

"I did. I think it was Biscuit,"

Chloe giggled. "Biscuit? That's a funny name."

"I'll tell you what, Chloe. I love biscuits and gravy, and I really love this horse, so—"

"You named him biscuit." Jolie clapped her hands and giggled along with Chloe. "I never had biscuits and gravy. Daddy gives us cereal most of the time."

"He makes pancakes sometimes. He puts Mickey Mouse ears on them and adds berries for the eyes, nose and mouth. Daddy is silly."

"I think your dad is a champ, Jolie.

Both girls tilted their heads at him as Chloe asked, "What's a champ?"

"A champ is a winner. Someone who is good at what he does and deserves good things."

Chloe skipped around him. "Our daddy deserves good things, and he got one really good thing."

Jolie eyed her. "What?"

"A wife, and we got a new mommy."

Jolie rocked her head back and forth. "Dumb me. I knew that."

"You're not dumb, Jolie." Grif's chest tightened, happy he'd halted that kind of talk. "Your mind wasn't in the same place with your sister."

"Right. I'm not dumb."

Air escaped his lungs as he tied off the string on their conversation. "These horses are anxious for their treats."

That did it. Both girls followed him, and insisted he introduce them. Jolie gave her apple to Biscuit, and Chloe stood at Russet's stall and held up the apple for him. While he feed Bandit, Jolie had shifted down to one of his smaller horses.

"Who's this littler one?" She gazed at him with wide eyes.

"She's a filly, which means a girl horse, and her name is Lady."

Chloe nestled closer to the gate. "Jolie and me will be ladies someday."

"You will be." Not wanting to get into the difference between girls, ladies and women, he stepped away from Lady's stall and shifted to the next. "This is Dusty. He's a man horse." He'd dug deep for that explanation. Stallion and Gelding would become too technical for him to explain.

"Okay, I think they all have a treat, so how about we go into the orchard with a basket and pick some apples that have fallen off the limbs."

"What's an orchard?" Jolie squinted at him, her nose scrunched.

Chloe pushed Jolie's shoulder. "You know. It means trees with fruit on them."

"You don't have to punch me, Chloe." Jolie gave her shoulder a whack. "Grandma has an orchard."

"You hit me. And grandma has only one tree that has cherries."

Grif's lack of experience took its toll as he grappled

with what to do. "Girls, no punching or pushing or hitting. No more, okay?"

They both drew back with wide eyes. "Okay."

Their echoed response caught him off-guard. They tended to speak as a duet...at least that's what he heard. "Many fruit trees make an orchard. Cherries can be part of an orchard and often are, so let's not worry about one or two trees now."

Two heads nodded, and he suspected they knew they had stepped too far. "Sorry." Jolie spoke first with Chloe her echo.

Dismissing his idea to put the horses in the corral, he wrangled the twins to the apple trees, each carrying a basket, and he breathed a sigh as they hurried from one spot to another to pick up the bruised apples that he used to feed the horses. While they did their job, he took time to round-up his creativity. The girls needed things to do, and he had to come up with fresh ideas.

When he eyed his watch, he couldn't believe that time hadn't even trotted. Time had lumbered along like a horse with a stone in its hoof. As the apples vanished from beneath the trees, their next task would be his original plan. The horses needed their exercise in the corral, and the girls would enjoy helping him move them there.

They stored the apples where he showed them, and as they did, he attached a rein on three horses. "Girls, let's take Dusty, Lady and Biscuit to the corral. Can you help me?"

Chloe dropped the apple basket so fast, it nearly tipped over and she darted to his side, her face glowing with the new adventure. Sometimes she reminded him of Ally when he'd first met her. She had been a woman who lived for new experiences, adventure and fun. Even more than Jolie, Chloe appeared to be the one who took on Ally's nature.

He gave Dusty's rein to Chloe and had her wait while he showed Jolie how to hold the rein as she walked Lady to the corral. He joined them with Biscuit. He took his time walking to the corral, not wanting to excite the horses. If they did, the girls wouldn't be able to contain them. With their first success, they returned and led Russet and Bandit to join the other two horses. Though it took a bit of time, he faced the slow-moving hour hand, and hoped he could find something for the girls to do inside. Later they could put the horses back in the stable.

"Let's go in, and we could have a treat. You did lots of work today."

Both nodded and skipped along beside him. After they were settled at the kitchen table with glasses of milk, he opened the paper bag and pulled out the healthy cookies that had given him a chuckle. They were piled in a plastic bag and beneath them, his pulse skipped when he saw a couple of decks of cards and another box. Dear Marcy had realized he would need help and sent something to entertain the girls.

"Look what I found." He held up the cards and the box. As he did, he noticed it was a jigsaw puzzle. "Do you like to do puzzles?

Both darted toward him with huge smiles. "We love puzzles." Chloe reached out for the box. "Jolie, it's a new one." She held it up so her twin could see the photo on the front.

Jolie faced him, pointing to the nice surprise. "Where can we make it? Do you have a place?"

Realizing it might take more than one sitting, he recalled an old card table he had stored in the laundry room. "How about a card table? That way you can keep it there if you don't finish it."

"Yeah!" Chloe danced around the room, and he looked heavenward, again thanking Marcy for her thoughtfulness.

"Here's the cookies." He set four of them on the paper plate he'd placed between them. "I'll get the card table while you have your milk and healthy cookies."

They didn't say a word, but they did grab for a cookie while he headed to the laundry room.

After work, Marcy headed home first to change her clothes and then ambled into the kitchen while she concocted a possible venture that she'd thought would give Grif a break. She checked her refrigerator and her small pantry and then stood for a moment to make her decision. She could do it.

With her plan in mind, she pulled out her phone and hit Grif's number, hoping she wasn't too late. When she heard his welcoming voice, she grinned. "Hi, Grif. How are you doing?"

"Marcy, you were a life saver. Thank you. I'm glad you realized I'm a newbie at caring for kids, especially two eager beavers like Jolie and Chloe. I was running out of activities until I gave them their cookie and milk treat and found the puzzle."

"Did they like it?"

"Like it? They loved it. I haven't had to do a thing for the past half-hour. I may go out and buy a few more."

"I'm glad, Grif. I thought of coloring books and

crayons too. Even I like to color."

He snickered. "Interesting."

"No, I'm not kidding. It's fun. Haven't you ever colored?" She pictured him leaning over a picture outline and going through the box of forty-eight colors to find the right one. "Everyone likes to—"

"Never in my life, really. Am I missing something?"

An idea flashed through her mind. "Time will tell."

"Okay, Marcy, that makes me nervous."

This time she tittered. "Coloring is not the reason I called."

"I'm glad. I suppose you wondered if I survived the day."

"Not exactly, but I wanted to help you out." Her pulse tripped, envisioning his expression.

"You already did. The cards and the puzzle. I had just reached the end of my creative ideas."

"I doubt it, but how's this. I'll make dinner and you can bring the girls over here instead of my coming to get them."

"Marcy, you don't have to—"

"I don't have to, but I want to. Nothing fancy, and I'm sure the girls like pasta."

"If they don't, I do. You're the best, Marcy. When do you want us?"

"Anytime. You can help me cook." Thinking of Grif beside her in the kitchen would have been a nightmare only months ago, but lately, his company and friendship had opened new doors for her. She loved how he made her feel.

Grif's laugh came over the phone. "You may have second thoughts after today."

"Never, Grif. Come anytime. I won't even insist on your cooking. You can set the table."

"I'm good at that."

She guessed that he was. "I'll see you when you get here, and thanks for saving me the trip."

"Thanks for saving me from cooking. I'll get the girls rounded up and we'll be there. soon."

As she hung up, she stood a moment, her eyes closed, surprised and yet not surprised that she'd been so bold to invite Grif for dinner. The girls visiting with him helped, but being comfortable with a man, toying with him, finding pleasure in his voice was something new—very new and totally out of her comfort level.

Yet, she'd acted on her feelings instead of hiding them, and that meant she had grown from the person she'd been when under her father's reign, and the person she could be today. She liked the new Marcy much better than the one cowering in the corner.

Chapter 4

Happy that Marcy had given the girls new coloring books and crayons, he stood alone with her in the kitchen helping her rinse the dishes as she placed them in the dishwasher. Seeing Marcy in her homey setting roused an unexpected comfortable feeling that edged through his body. In her company, an edgy sense of confusion often settled into his head, but today, he relaxed and for once felt at home.

"The pasta was really great, Marcy. You did something different to it, but I'm not sure what."

"Nothing that unusual, really." She glanced his way with a faint grin. "I like herbs and I added a couple that might not be in commercial pasta sauces. I add a bit of marjoram and a dash of ginger, and sometimes I add a little red wine."

"That's the wonderful flavor then. It's different and it's great."

"Thanks, Grif. I cook for so few people that I never know what people think."

"Well, you do now. You have talents you don't even know." He shook his head. "You're like one of those hidden treasures that is finally discovered."

Her expression changed, and he wished he'd kept

his mouth shut. "Did I say something wrong? If I did—
"

Marcy's palm flexed as if to stop him. "Grif, you said nothing wrong. You said something I've never heard before. In fact, I grew up thinking the opposite. If I'd been a treasure, it would have been one that should have stayed buried."

Grif jerked back. He opened his mouth and then closed it. What could he say, and why would

Marcy even think such a thing?

She eyed him a moment with a look he couldn't identify, as if she'd run into a brick wall and couldn't move.

"Grif, I'm upset with myself. I shouldn't have said what I did when you were trying to pay me a very kind compliment. I'm not used to them, I guess."

He longed to ask why. "No need to apologize, Marcy. Just know that I think you're a kind and generous woman." What would make her think that she was useless and not worth anything? He managed to contain his shock and let her comment slide. Yet, he wanted to know.

As she finished putting the dishes in the washer, he stepped back. "Can I do anything else in here? If not, I'll go and check on the girls. They're quiet."

"I'm fine. Thanks. You go and check on them, and I'll be done here in a minute."

He longed to stay, but he sensed she needed time to catch her breath and resolve what was bothering her. Or maybe he was wrong.

The closer he got to the girls, he only heard a couple of giggles. When he entered the living room, they were spread out on the floor with crayons spread across the carpet as they colored the pictures. He stood over them, amazed at the nice job they had done.

"You two are good colorers."

They tilted their heads upward and grinned. "We learned to stay in the lines when we were five." Chloe held up her book and showed him.

"Very nice, but I also like the colors."

Jolie didn't let Chloe take all the glory as she raised her picture. "We learned how to color with the right colors when we were five, too. See the sky is blue and the grass is green."

"And a pretty color green, Jolie. Just like it looks outside."

She nodded and went back to her crayons.

He settled on the couch and crossed his feet, enjoying the quiet. When he could talk with Marcy privately, he would ask where she purchased the coloring books and crayons. He wanted to have them handy on the ranch. Picking apples wouldn't last forever.

Marcy appeared at the doorway and stood a moment watching the girls. She gave him a thumbs up, and he nodded. "Everything's cleaned up and put away."

"Again, Marcy, thanks for the dinner."

He patted the cushion beside him, hoping she'd be close enough from them to have conversation without disturbing the quiet.

She stood a moment before moving closer and settling beside him.

They sat in silence for a while, listening to the girls discuss colors and watching them stay in the lines until he couldn't contain himself any longer.

"Where did you buy the crayons and books?" He tilted his head toward the girls.

"Drugs stores have them sometimes and dollar stores, but Wal-Mart has many choices if you want to pick up a couple for…"

He gave a nod before she finished. "Right. That's my plan."

"Good idea."

Her indifferent expression caused him to frown. "I'll pick some up tomorrow. I'm running out of ideas. But not to ignore your gifts—the puzzle and cards. Thanks again."

"You're welcome, Grif." She chuckled, and he didn't understand what caused it.

He reviewed what had been said, and nothing seemed funny. But when he gave up guessing and turned to her, she only studied him as if they'd just met.

Finally, she leaned back against the cushion and released a long breath. "For some reason, we're behaving like two strangers who just met a few minutes ago and were left alone with no idea what to talk about."

"Yep, that's it. I was thinking the same thing. What's going on?"

"I'm not sure, Grif. I said some things that I normally don't say to anyone, and I think it made me uncomfortable. And I'm guessing you're just confused as I am."

"You hit it, Marcy. Neither of us is used to sitting." He pointed to the girls, since the term babysitting didn't fit seven-year-olds.

She nodded. "It's not so bad though, is it?"

"No, it's not. I've found it challenging and I like an

occasional challenge." His relationship with Marcy had elements of a challenge since he had never dated or spent time with a woman. She'd become his guinea pig. The phrase knotted his chest. She'd become his test.

"I'm glad. If either of us find ourselves thinking of marri..." Her voice faded. "Getting involved with someone who has children, this would be good training."

"I suppose so." Marriage and being involved were two very different things as far as he was concerned. "Have you ever been involved with anyone, Marcy?"

"No. Never had the opportunity, I suppose."

Opportunities were always somewhere in a person's life. More likely she never gave an opportunity a chance. "I'm guessing you closed your eyes to chances."

"Not really. I just walked away. Chances or opportunities didn't appeal to me. I never saw a relationship that I cared to experience."

His forehead pulled upward as his eyes widened. She'd given him a hint of her background. Had she lived in an unloving environment or one even worse. Maybe volatile? "I didn't think about it much. I had a mom and dad who got along okay. They each had their jobs and did them. Mom raised us because dad worked long hours, and Mom trained us to help around the house. We earned privileges for the tasks we completed. Sometimes a little money. Nothing special, but nothing negative either.

She closed her eyes and lowered her head.

"I'm sorry you saw behaviors that put you on edge to forming relationships, Marcy. That wasn't fair to you."

"Maybe I'm too sensitive, Grif. I'm not fond of talking about it so…"

He understood and muzzled his head full of questions. "No need. Let's talk about something else. For example, would you like to learn more about horses? The ranch is interesting, and you might enjoy experiencing what it's like to live on a ranch."

A faint grin stole across her face. "You sound like Ally. She is always approaching me with new experiences, and…" She shrugged. "I suppose there's no harm in learning something new."

"Learning is important. It makes us well-rounded people. I'm guessing you can teach me some things too. I'm sure you could give me some cooking lessons."

She brushed his words away with a laugh. "Me?"

"Listen, you had secret ingredients in the pasta sauce. Doesn't that make you a master chef."

Her face lit up brighter than he's seen it that day. "I'll think about that, Grif. Really. Maybe that's my calling."

He reached across his knees and placed his hand over hers as he gave it a squeeze. Nothing else was said, but she hadn't pulled away, and he let his hand linger over hers, enjoying the closeness, and hoping that their conversation, though uneasy, had opened doors for both of them.

♥

The next day, Marcy hoped to catch Ally at work, curious about the invitation she'd received from her for dinner. Since Ally had married, she'd been tied up with the settling into Cade's ranch house and probably making it her own, as well as spending time with the girls and Cade. On top of that she worked five days a week.

Marcy couldn't imagine being that busy and in demand. But then Ally had always been a woman looking for excitement and adventure…although usually she wanted it to be fun. But then maybe spending time with the girls and Cade was fun.

She'd accepted and now she looked in her closet to decide what to wear. Was it casual or dress-up or… The "or" caught her. What else but in costume, and she knew it wasn't any time near Halloween.

Looking at her dresses and skirts, she gave up and chose casual. Ally lived on a ranch so she would stick with that idea. She located her best denim slacks, a bit dressier than jeans, and a comfortable knit top with a scoop neckline. Perhaps she could tie a neckerchief around her neck and add a western flair.

She giggled at herself as she found a coordinating color in an interesting print and tied it in a loose knot around her neck. Not bad and if it bothered her after she arrived, she could slip it off and drop it in her purse.

Her cosmetics caused no grief. She wore little and added a blush, a daub of mascara and picked up a tube and slid an orange shade along her lips. She straightened the vanity, grabbed her shoulder bag and headed toward the living room.

Though she'd planned to drive, Grif called and said he'd been invited and knew she was going so he offered to drive. She'd welcomed the invitation. Though she usually had to drive at night, winding her way back to Cottonwood from the Village of Oak Creek wasn't her favorite.

Ally insisted she bring nothing for the meal, so she gave in, but tossed a couple of miniature puzzles into her oversized shoulder bag for the twins. Taking something along made her feel better.

Instead of waiting inside, she stepped onto the condo porch and sat on a canvas chair. The sun spread its rays across the strip of grass, and she watched a few insects fly around some colorful flowers they seemed to like.

Ally would call her life boring and would never find insects an adventure or fun. Marcy shook her head. She'd refused so many events that Ally had tried to lure her to attend or try. She'd avoided a hot air balloon ride, learning to horseback ride and too many other "adventures" to count.

Grif's wheels crunched on the gravel and she rose before he got out of the car, but it was too late. He waited for her and then followed her around to the passenger side and opened the door. She'd never get used to his cavalier nature.

She smiled as he stepped back. "Thanks, Grif. You always surprise me."

"I do." He arched his left eye brow. "I'm glad. I like surprises."

After she slipped into the car, Grif closed her door and returned to the driver's seat. "You look very nice, Marcy. I like you in that color, although I'm not good at knowing the names. It looks a little like the color of a ripe peach, a pink-orange color. You should wear that more often."

Words caught in her throat, and she choked trying to get them out. "I've never been a ripe peach. I hope that's good." She managed a grin.

He reached across the distance and touched her arm. "It's more than good, Marcy."

Her lungs emptied, and she could only smile at him. When the air returned to her lungs, she asked him the question that had hung in her mind. "Do you know what this dinner is all about?"

"I'm guessing it's a thank you for being part of their wedding and taking care of the kids while they were gone the three days."

"Ah, I didn't think of that." She shook her head. "I'm always looking for some hidden meaning since I've spent my time with Ally dodging her creative ideas for me."

"Don't be distrustful. You know, Ally finds things fun, and doesn't understand people who don't..." His voice faded. "Although you never know until you try things, Marcy. You might love a couple things that Ally has suggested."

Her jaw dropped, hearing Grif side with Ally. She thought he knew her fairly well now, but she'd been totally wrong.

When she didn't respond, Grif's expression sank to something similar to a frown. Maybe he was confused. She was.

They rode in silence for a while, until the conversation moved into a noncommittal topic. He talked about the ranch, and she mentioned a few incidents at work. Before long, they'd followed the roundabout to Jack's Canyon Road and headed up toward Cade's ranch.

When they pulled up, she was surprised to see another car, but that was none of her business. For some reason she thought, as she and Grif had discussed, that the dinner was for their part in the wedding and caring for the children those few days.

Grif opened the door for her and said nothing about the other car, so she didn't either. When they entered the house, her confusion ended. "Hi Rachel, nice to see you." The woman she greeted worked with her at the hospital.

"Marcy." Rachel stood and opened her arms. "Since moving to another floor, I rarely see you. I was pleased when Ally invited me to the ranch and said you were coming too."

"I had no idea you were invited, but it's great to see you." Marcy shifted her gaze to Ally, asking herself why Ally hadn't mentioned Rachel.

Ally caught the drift because she shifted to face Marcy. "I'm sorry. I thought I told you. Rachel and Don were coming. They love to ride horses so we thought it would be fun to…" She stumbled over her words as guilt slid over her face. "I forgot, Marcy. I'm so sorry."

Rachel frowned. "Forgot what?"

Ally drew in a breath. "Marcy doesn't ride, but everyone else does. We'll work it out." She appeared to brush it away, but her faux pas was obvious, and Marcy's discomfort couldn't be hidden.

"Please enjoy the appetizers, and let Cade know what you two want to drink." Ally waved her hands wildly. "I need to check on dinner before it's burned."

Cade shook his head as he approached Grif. "Listen, we don't have to all go out for a ride. I don't mind staying back with Marcy and the rest of you go. It won't be a long ride anyway, and—"

Grif dropped his hand on Cade's shoulder. "Don't apologize. It was an ordinary idea. This is a horse ranch. We're not offended." He glanced in Marcy's direction, and she put on the best pleasant face she could muster.

It wasn't like Ally to hurt her feelings or even try to belittle her, although that's how she felt. Ally had bugged her about learning to ride and she'd resent her pressure as always. If Ally wanted to bungee jump off a bridge, she seemed to assume that Marcy should want to join her.

Ally's personal goals had always been to have fun and experience excitement until she fell in love with Cade and his twin's, Chloe and Jolie. Then the girls became her excitement and sometimes it was real excitement. She remembered the day, they were dog sitting and when the dog followed a quail into the meadow, the girls followed too and ended up stranded on a ledge of Wild Horse Mesa.

When the conversation shifted, and she sat on the sofa next to Grif, she leaned close to his ear and whispered her thanks. It took him a minute to give her a nod, but she knew he understood.

She sipped her lemonade and slipped in a little conversation with Rachel and Don, although their interest settled around the horse ranch and the breeds of horses Cade owned. She knew little about horses and with some of her time hanging out with Grif, learning about ranch life and horses made sense. Horseback riding didn't, however.

Ally stepped into the room and announced dinner. Cade rose and gestured toward the doorway. Rachel and Don followed Ally as did Cade, and she and Grif took their time. In that alone moment, she touched his arm. "I'm so sorry, Grif. I feel guilty, as if I'm ruining everyone's fun, and especially—"

"Marcy, please. Ally didn't mean anything, I'm sure, and you haven't ruined anyone's fun. I have a ranch, too, and I can ride anytime I want so it's not important to me."

"But I fear—"

"Let's get in there, and we can talk about it later." He gave her a wink, and she plastered a grin on her face and stepped into the dining room.

Once settled, they filled their plates and the conversation moved from the ranches to the hospital and to the lovely weather they'd been having. Horseback riding didn't come into the conversation, and yet to her, it was as if a stallion stood in the dining room that no one mentioned. She'd put a damper on the event.

That had been her life. She'd let her upbringing hang onto her adult life. The time had come that she make a change. A big change. But how?

♥

Grif moved the food around on his plate and managed to eat most of it, but his stomach had knotted sensing the hurt that Marcy had felt. Ally had always been a good friend to her, and he couldn't believe her thoughtfulness had been on purpose, but Marcy's sensitivity made it seem that way. He wished he understood why she lived on the edge of a cliff as if waiting to be pushed off.

"This chicken is delicious, Ally."

Marcy's comment took him by surprise. She'd been very quiet since the riding comment, and he was proud of her for giving Ally a compliment. The chicken was excellent with the perfect amount of herbs and a tender and juicy consistency.

Before he could agree, everyone committed on what he had just thought. The sparse conversation grew as they finished their meal, and they all voted to hold off on dessert until later and headed back to the living room.

Before he reached the doorway, Marcy had gathered a few of the dishes and headed for the kitchen, but Ally stopped her. "Thanks, Marcy, but I can do this. Please, go back and enjoy yourself with the others. You're my company."

"I know that, but I'm your friend, and what are friends for? I think I've heard you say that." Without doing as Ally said, she marched into the kitchen with the dishes.

Grif avoided the situation and followed the others into the living room more confused than usual. He thought he'd begun to know Marcy, but, apparently, he knew nothing. That grated him and left him deep in thought as to what he could do to help her know her worth. But then maybe helping a friend was her worth. He thought about spending the three days with Cade's girls.

He drew in a breath and tried to concentrate on the conversation between Cade and the other couple which lead them to the idea to go out to the stable and select the horses they would ride.

Though Cade beckoned him to follow, he couldn't go and leave Marcy in the kitchen. He'd never been a man who got edgy about things, but today he was. He didn't like the feeling of uncertainty. How could he handle the situation? Marcy would insist he go riding, but he had no plan to leave her alone while everyone left. If he had known what the dinner would lead to, he would have never accepted the invitation.

When Marcy came into the living room, she faltered in the doorway and looked around. "Where is everyone?"

He lifted a shoulder. "Out to look at the horses."

"Oh." She ambled across the room and plopped into a chair nearby. "I was thinking about that. Since you have a horse ranch, I should try to learn a little bit about horses. I know nothing."

His pulse skipped, almost believing she'd read his mind. "Great plan. I'd love telling you about the breeds and anything else you'd like to know."

She gave a nod. "I don't know much about anything other than cleaning a house and cooking."

"Don't say that, Marcy. You work in a hospital. You know about patient care, and you were great with the twins, so you know about keeping kids busy and safe. Why not give yourself credit for what you can do?"

"Be seen and not heard. Isn't that a woman's role?"

A weight pressed against his chest as he gazed at her disbelieving what she'd said. "No, it's not. A woman's role is to be a person who explores life just as a man does, who often falls in love and gets married, who has children and is a mother. Who has a career, just as you do, Marcy. Where did you get that idea?"

She appeared to pale, and he wanted to withdraw what he'd said, but it was too late. "Marcy, I'm sorry, but you startled me. No one on earth should be seen and not heard. No one."

She lowered her head a moment, and when she lifted her chin, tears rimmed her eyes. "I wish you could have explained that to my father."

"Your father?" Air escaped his lungs. "Do you mean that's what you were taught?"

She only nodded her head, her eyes focused on something off in the distance. "It was my way of life...and my mother's."

What kind of a man would treat his family so horridly? But he couldn't ask that question. "Maybe that's how your father was schooled, Marcy. But how ever he learned that rule, he was wrong. No one should be seen and not heard. Not even children. Yes, they need rules to be polite and speak in appropriate ways, but not to live without being heard. Never."

His stomach ached witnessing the deep hurt in her expression. That kind of training caused her to be a woman afraid to try anything new or different, afraid to speak out and express an opinion, afraid of living. She deserved so much more.

Grif rose and crossed to the chair where Marcy sat. He reached down and eased her into his arms, drawing her close. He held her tight, praying that what he'd said entered her mind and heart as deeply as he cared about her.

He'd never fallen in love, but Marcy had become special to him. Was it love? He didn't know what that kind of love felt like, but he knew he cared about her, and he wanted to help her become the woman she had been meant to be.

Marcy clung to him, an occasion ripple of emotion caused her to tremble, and he suspected tears were filling her eyes, but he saw no need to investigate. Instead he held her in his arms with the hope that she would understand how much he cared.

When she drew back, he saw he'd been correct. Her

misty eyes gazed at him with a kind of gratitude he'd never experienced. He had a mission, and he would follow it. Marcy would become a whole woman and no longer being only a shadow who lived in fear of breaking her father's rules.

His heart still heavy, Grif managed to shift his emotion to purpose. "Let's go outside and look at the horses. You can begin your lesson today. How does that sound?"

"I-I'm not sure about a lesson, but I can enjoy seeing you ride, Grif. That would make me happy."

Always, Marcy found joy in other people's happiness and never looked for her own. That would end. "Good. That's a beginning of learning about horses, isn't it?"

She nodded, but as he steered her toward the door, his own plan formed in his head, a plan that needed subtlety and yet firmness.

He slipped his hand into hers as they headed for the stable. Though he'd anticipated her pulling away, she didn't, and his confidence grew. Marcy trusted him, and though he didn't want to destroy the trust, he prayed they could make progress toward helping her be comfortable around the horses.

When they arrived, Cade had already helped the others tack the horses, and Grif encouraged them to start their rides. When Rachel started a conversation with Marcy, he took Cade off to the side and asked him which horse would be the best for a new rider. Cade gave him a wink, letting him know he understood, and recommended Dixie, a mare quarter-horse.

"I'll be behind you. Have fun." He called out to the foursome who headed toward the meadow in the direction of Wild Horse Mesa.

After they waved goodbye, he led Marcy along the stalls and paused by Dixie. "Here's a young lady who is gentle and good for new riders. Whenever you're ready to learn, she would be a good one. Lady would be a good one for a new rider at my ranch."

He shifted without pressing the point and stopped at Snickers who had been left behind. "I'll saddle up this one for me. He's a fine horse too."

She didn't respond but didn't back away. Her acceptance gave him hope. He gathered the tack and begin the process of saddling Snickers. As he did, he explained the step-by-step process to Marcy.

"What do you think?" He paused and grinned. "This is your first lesson. You know the names of the tack and where it goes on the horse."

"And you expect me to remember?"

"Not totally. Let's test you." He lifted the reins and tilted his head.

"Reins. That was easy."

"How about this?" He pointed.

"Stirrups. I put the ball of my foot here on the stirrup and point my toe outward." She smiled.

He squeezed her shoulder. "You're a good learner. Perfect. How about if I saddle up Dixie and just let you sit on her. No riding. What do you say?"

She drew in a lengthy breath and turned her head toward him as the air left her lungs. "Is this a trick? You'll hit the horse's rump, and I'll be sailing across the meadow…" She lowered her head. "I'm sorry, Grif. I know you wouldn't do that."

"I'm glad you trust me, Marcy."

Her tense expression relaxed. "Again, I'm sorry.

Why don't you mount Snickers, and I'll watch you a little while first?"

First. His hopes rose. Did she mean if he looked at ease, she might give it a try? He could only hope.

He slipped his foot into the stirrup and hoisted himself onto the saddle. She stood back and watched. Instead of trotting off, he signaled Snickers to walk a few steps toward the meadow. The Appaloosa moved forward as he'd asked, and he guided him into the meadow then, he steered back around toward Marcy. "What do you say?"

She patted the horse's mane. "He minds well."

"I think Cade said that Bliss is very gentle, maybe even more than Dixie. Could I saddle her up, and you can give her a try?" He studied Marcy's face, noting various emotions merging from one to the other.

"I don't know, Grif. I really don't mind if you go ahead and catch up with the others and I'll—"

"You'll do nothing of the sort. Either we both go or we both stay." He hated putting her in that position, but motivation could work wonders.

She gazed up at him, her hand brushing the horse's shoulder. "You're putting me on the spot."

"No, I said I'm willing to stay back with—"

She gave a fast head shake. "But I want you to ride with—"

"Now, you're putting me on the spot. Think about it." He gazed at her, his heart aching for her and the pressure he'd created, but she needed something and he prayed the conversation would motivate her to take a chance. To trust him. To just get on the saddle if that's all she could handle.

She didn't say a word, but her gaze did. Her eyes

scanned the horse from head to tail, her head tilting from one direction to another until finally her arms dropped at her side, and her gaze moved to him. "Okay, I'll get on the saddle, but…"

"But the rest is up to you, Marcy. I mean that."

She lowered her gaze. "Okay."

He worked fast before she changed her mind, and when Belle was saddled, he led her outside the stable to Marcy.

Marcy ran her hand over the horse's coat, touched the reins and eyed the stirrup. "I start with my left foot, right?"

"Correct."

She stared at the stirrup for a moment, moved forward and slipped her toe into the strap stopping when the ball of her foot hit the mark.

He gave her a glowing smile—one from the heart. She'd listened and learned. She hoisted her right leg over the saddle and slipped her right foot into the stirrup. When she grasped the reins, Bliss took a step, Marcy loosened her grip as panic rose on her face. But Bliss understood, and Marcy's panic vanished when she laughed. "Bliss does understand doesn't she. I didn't mean to give the reins a little tug, but I think I did."

"But she paused and waited for more direction. You did the right thing by loosening the rein. You let her know not to move."

"Good." She smiled. "But the step wasn't bad at all. Could I try a couple of steps with her?"

"I'll ride along beside you, Marcy, and you do as I told you. Leg pressure and the reins are both signals. You can even say, Whoa, and Bliss will understand."

"Really?"

He nodded and couldn't help but chuckle. "Horses are smart when they're trained. And Bliss is gentle too." He watched her study the reins and gaze at her knees.

"So, if I want to go slowly, I can just do a small movement on the reins. Right?"

"Right. And I'll be with you."

She sat a moment before she acted on her impulse to give riding a try.

When she did, Bliss stepped forward in a walk, and he followed, adding a compliment to Bliss and to her as they stepped further away from the stable and eventually arrived at the open field of grass.

He didn't push trotting, but that would work for another lesson. One of these days, Marcy would be a cowgirl...maybe a careful one, but she would be able to ride. His spirit lifted, seeing the delight on her face.

When she turned his way, a grin brightened her face. "Thank you, Grif. I would never have done this without you, and now I wonder what other things I might learn so I can enjoy life without the fear of..." She lifted her shoulders.

His heart warmed with her look. "Fear of being seen but not heard. You'll be able to be seen and heard now, Marcy. And you should be. You're a great woman who's been stifled too long. I'm honored to have your trust and watch you become the woman you have always been inside but afraid to let it out."

Tears rolled down her cheeks, and he wished he hadn't said so much, but her soft voice reached him. "Grif, thank you more than I can say."

Chapter 5

Marcy's head spun as she pictured herself on horseback. She'd never tried anything, but Grif, with kindness, had encouraged her to try it, and she hated to disappoint him. Maybe that was good. If she hadn't tried, she would never know what she could do.

Grif had invited her to come over for a few lessons, and though her old fears returned, she made herself agree that she would be there. If she could care for two active seven-year-olds for a few days, who knew what other things she could accomplish.

The image that remained in her memory caused her to flounder as she faced the truth she hated to admit. Her father had been cruel. She'd grown up thinking her father's words were typical of a dad. Now, she'd learned that they were not. They were self-serving to keep his power over her and her mom. If she'd had siblings, they might have been able to join forces and rebel against her father's demands, but she had none...or did she?

Her mother had slipped once on the telephone while speaking to a friend and hadn't realized that she had been within hearing distance. If she hadn't gasped, her mother may have never known that she overheard the conversation.

But her mother never talked about the shocking secret even when Marcy tried to bring up the subject. After seeing the expression on her mother's face, she'd always wished she hadn't. Yet she'd spent her life time trying to figure out if she'd heard her mother correctly and what the startling news meant, but she'd left the recollection sit deep in her brain. With her mom gone, she may never understand or know the answer.

Her father's unkind words filled her mind, and she wondered if he'd done something bad, but everything had been so vague, and she'd been young. Still the thought lingered. Even though curious, she had never wanted to talk about it with anyone. Not even Ally.

Back at work, she'd had a chance to speak with Ally, and rather than being manipulated into one of Ally's wild ideas, for once it turned out to be a fun conversation. She couldn't help but grin, when Ally expressed the excitement that she'd seen her on horseback.

Knowing Ally's continual encouragement, she could now imagine other of Ally's images of her in a hot air balloon, bungee jumping or parachuting from an airplane. Marcy prayed the horseback incident would not stimulate Ally's drive to push her to try more new experiences.

Though Ally had been a good friend for a long time, Marcy struggled now, since she'd found the new Marcy within the quiet and stunted being she'd been, whether she and Ally could remain close. She had begun to learn to stand up for herself and to run her own life and not let others push her around. She had lived with other people's pressure for too long. But not Grif. He encouraged but never pressured her to do what he wanted.

Grif, in her mind, caused a smile to tug her face. She'd promised to drop by, and she'd decided to follow through while she was at work. Though facing the possibility of what he might want her to do, she did hesitate and yet grasped the confidence she had in him to give her room to be herself.

He'd mention having another person for a lesson in the early afternoon and suggested she could come to the ranch later...after work. She'd thought to bring a change of clothes rather than drive home first. She slipped into her jeans, and a comfortable top in the employees' restroom, preparing to go. He'd suggested later...and now was later.

Pleased that he'd encouraged her to visit him at the ranch, she couldn't stop the smile that stayed on her face. Something about Grif brightened her day. She'd never known anyone like him. Grif was special in so many ways. Her chest tightened picturing him on horseback, his shirt framing his broad chest, his strong hands holding the reins, and the special look he gave her.

She said goodnight to the staff and hurried to the parking lot. With fall approaching, she enjoyed the cooler temperature even with a bright sun shining on the hills and mesas on the way to Grif's ranch. Meadows through Cottonwood stretched from the highway to rugged mountains in the distance, and an occasional cactus dominated the view, the Sequoia with its arms raised toward the blue sky.

When she turned into the ranch driveway, she saw a car sitting back by the barn. Apparently, the other lesson was still in progress. She pulled beside the car and sat there not knowing what to do, but after a while, she opened the door and stepped onto the grass, thinking he might be unsaddling the horse in the stable.

She headed that way, and when she entered, the stable was empty except for the usual horses gazing at her from their stalls. the lesson had to be over. Laughing at herself, she headed to the house. Why would Grif sit outside and wait for her. Naturally he was inside.

When she reached the door, she glanced through the screen and as she reached up to knock, she heard voices. Laughter actually. A woman's laugh and Grif's mingled with hers. She drew back, confused about what to do. He'd never mentioned another woman, but then why would he?

She turned away from the door, and as she did, she heard Grif call her name. Faltering she wavered with what to do, respond or keep going. She hurried down the first stair as the door opened and Grif stepped out with a blank stare that grew to a frown.

"Where are you going?" He rubbed the back of his neck, his gaze glued to hers.

"You're busy, and I didn't want to interfere. You said you had a lesson today and—"

"Marcy, the lesson's over. I'm just talking with Betsy. I know her from the store. You're not interrupting at all."

"But I didn't know if—"

"If what?" He shook his head. "Betsy's the daughter of a family who owned a ranch in Cottonwood, but when her dad died, her mother sold the ranch, and they moved to Phoenix where Betsy's brother lives."

"I'm sorry, Grif, I…"

"Betsy misses the horses and riding. She asked if I could give her some pointers since it's been such a long time since she's ridden. She's getting married and her husband plans to buy a ranch."

Marcy's stomach knotted while Grif stared at her, explaining who the woman was. An old long-time friend who was getting married. Shame washed over her, and she opened her mouth to apologize again, but she'd already done that. "I'd like to meet her."

"I'd planned that you would." He stepped back and opened the door, motioning for her to enter, and though she wanted to crawl in or fall through the floor, she walked in as if she hadn't made a fool of herself. What was she thinking? But she knew.

When she entered, an attractive young woman, probably in her late twenties rose. "Hi, I'm Betsy. Grif told me you'd be here so I waited. I wanted to meet you. You and Grif seem to be good friends, and I like hearing that."

Marcy stuck out her hand. "I just heard about you, Betsy. I'm Marcy White, a new student of Grif's trying to learn how to ride a horse…sort of."

Betsy chuckled, her face lighting the room. "He said you're not one to try new things, and he's proud of you for your willingness to learn more about horses and riding."

"Proud? Wow, I didn't know that." She turned her head to smile at Grif. "He is a man of patience."

The young woman nodded with another titter. "That's why I learned more from him than my dad. Dad assumed everyone should just climb on a horse and ride, as if we were born that way."

"Not me. I'm a coward."

"No, you're smart. A person can get hurt thinking they can be a good rider without knowing something about horses and how to work with them." Betsy's expression took on a more serious look. "I had a friend who thought she could ride without knowing what she was doing, and she was thrown off the horse and cracked her head on a rock. She went through all kinds of treatments to bring her back to normal. Using wisdom, listening to your instructor and taking it slow, that's what is smart." She turned and eyed Grif. "Isn't that right?"

"Sure is, Bets." He gave a nod, and when he turned to Marcy, he motioned to the living room chairs. "Marcy have a seat. I'm sorry. I'm not sure what happened to my manners."

"It's not you, Grif. You have great manners." She grinned. "I'm the one who's a bit slow." She crossed to an easy chair and sat.

Betsy remained standing. "Listen Grif, I need to get going, but I thank you so much for the practice. Another hour or so, I should be able to remember all I knew once."

"You did fine, Bets. Just let me know when you want to come, and congratulations on the upcoming wedding. I'm really happy for you."

"You'll be invited, Grif, so I'll see you then too." She turned toward Marcy. "It's so nice meeting you Marcy, and I'm happy to see that Grif's finally in the land of the living. He's been a loner … in a way." She turned to him. "Right?"

He nodded.

"I think you've been a good influence on his life."

"He's been a good influence on me, too, Betsy. I think we'd both agree he's a special man."

"For sure." She picked up her bag from the floor and gave a wave as she headed for the doorway. "See you soon, Grif. I'm anxious for you to meet Craig." She paused looking at her. "I hope to see you again too, Marcy." With a wave, she stepped outside and was gone.

Marcy stared at the door, disbelieving the jealousy that had weighted her chest and her imagination. Why had she assumed, Betsy was Grif's lady friend? He'd never spoken about any women in his life. In fact, he'd been fairly clear that he'd been what Betsy stated, a loner most of the time. His best friend seemed to be Cade.

When she focused on Grif, he remained thoughtful. The stir she had caused made her feel ridiculous. How could she explain it? She'd never been jealous of another woman. Never.

Before she could decide how to approach her discomfort, Grif shifted to the couch and patted the seat beside him. "Let's talk."

His comment struck her chest like a wild tennis ball. She ambled toward him and sat, leaving a noticeable distance between him. She needed time to think and get her warped mind under control.

They sat in silence until she could remain quiet no longer. "Grif, I don't know what got into me. I have no excuse for acting so strange. I—"

"Marcy, please." Grif shifted closer to her and slipped his hand over hers. "Please don't apologize. You don't have to explain."

Yet she longed to give him a reason, if she could

only understand herself.

He sat in silence, the fingers of his free hand tapping on his knee, and she sensed his discomfort. Marcy blamed herself despite his insistence that she didn't need to explain. The quiet thundered in her head.

Grif shifted on the cushion as he turned to face her. "We have a lot to talk about. I know it's difficult for you sometimes, but it's not easy for me either, so I'm just going to jump in and open the trunk."

The trunk? When she opened her mouth to ask, the meaning struck her. She had a trunk too. The place where all her emotions and feelings stayed put.

Grif cleared his throat, his gaze drifting from one place to another until he stopped and sat still. "I don't like the tension I feel sometimes, Marcy. I know that has been your problem too. You and I set goals for ourselves or maybe non-goals for ourselves. Men and women, who are in the stage of their lives when they want to feel settled, often open themselves up to what used to be called the dating game." He shook his head. "I know that's an ancient phrase."

She nodded. "But I know what you mean. I see that in action all the time, but..."

"But it's not where your mind has been, Marcy. I know that. And neither has mine. For many years, I settled into my small world filled with horses, the store and the upkeep of the ranch. I didn't need anything else. My life was full and so was my time."

"Your life has been much different than mine, Grif. I didn't have horses or a ranch or much anything but an apartment and a job at the hospital. I don't even have a family. Dad died years ago, and Mom's been gone for a while now."

"So, what motivated your life, Marcy? What did you look forward too? How did you spend your time and use your talents?"

"We already know I don't really have talents, although you have already argued that." She somehow managed to send him a grin. "I looked forward to getting home from work and seeing a new day. My long-term plans were to travel one day, but I had no one to travel with, so those were more like dreams than real plans."

"And no marriage or children plans?" He already knew the answer. He'd heard a bit about her father and her parents' marriage.

"No. Never. I like kids but I've never envisioned myself confident with them. You remember our time with the twins. I tried, but I always doubted myself. Being a parent is one of the most difficult jobs in the world. That's how I see it."

"Difficult, but rewarding." Grif watched her expression shift from determination to confusion. "Can you see any rewards of having a child or two?"

She shrugged, her eyes aimed at the floor.

"How about your legacy? That's when I began to question my attitude. When I am gone, what will I leave on this earth? Who will take over the store, the ranch and the horses? Who will..." He faltered, suspecting Marcy had no interest in legacy.

She lifted her head. "I never thought about that. Not ever. I have nothing to leave the world. My apartment is rented. I don't own expensive jewelry or anything else. I didn't create anything wonderful like a book of poetry, a novel or painting. Nothing. So, who would care?"

"I would." The words flew from his mind to his tongue.

Marcy jolted upward. "You? But why, Grif? As you said, you have much to give. Much to leave for someone, so you are the one who needs a place or person to leave it to."

Grif swallowed, unsure of his decision. "Marcy, you might be upset about this, but I have to say it. You give yourself no credit. You don't see the good things that you are or the fine things that you do."

"Grif, I—"

"Marcy, please let me finish." He flinched when she pulled back as if someone had yanked her from behind. "You didn't see yourself with Chloe and Jolie, but I did. You were wonderful with them. You were creative and thoughtful. Attentive. Gentle. You were filled with motherly attributes that you learned from somewhere."

She drew up her shoulder in a lengthy breath he feared would be an angry rebuttal. She looked away and then directed her eyes to his. "I didn't learn that from my mother, but I don't blame her, really. She had little chance to be the kind of person she wanted to be."

"Your father had the power. I understand. But I need to ask you something."

Her eyes widened before she gave a nod. "Go ahead."

"Am I anything like your father?" Tension knotted along his shoulders and ached in his neck.

"You know the answer to that. No. Nothing like him."

"Then you don't believe that all men are like your father."

She searched his face as if trying to read his mind. "That's right. Cade is a wonderful father and a good husband. You would be an amazing dad and husband, Grif. I'm not a hater of men. I'm just cautious."

"So am I, but from the time I met you, I saw hints of your special attributes, and yet, I couldn't understand why you were so quiet and almost fearful of letting the real Marcy out of the box. But as time has passed and you have opened to me, I can see those many wonderful traits, and I know that you would be a treasure as a wife and mother. I want you to believe me."

"Why?" Her eyes captured his.

"Don't you know? Because I care about you more than I can say, and I hope that you have feelings for me too. I would love to hear you say that you do."

"Grif, I do care about you. Very much. I'm damaged in many ways. My head is filled with all kinds of memories that I don't understand and things I wish I could forget. I don't want to drag those horrors into a relationship and ruin someone's life."

He rose and drew Marcy up into his arms. "But I want to be the man to help you forget and forgive and overcome those horrors. That's my goal, and don't ask why, because I just told you how much I care."

She pressed her face into his shoulder while her body trembled with emotions that he wished she could have buried long ago, but he didn't know her story, so who was he to judge? Marcy's tears dampened his shirt, and he held her tight, rubbing small circles on her back below her neck and wishing he could rub away her pain. He didn't want to let her go.

Chapter 6

Marcy struggled to stop her flow of tears. For too many years, she'd hidden away memories and hurts that she'd allowed to cling to her and make her someone she didn't want to be. She thanked the Lord that Grif had stepped into her life. His kindness and concern meant the world to her. Yet the relationship left her with fear. What would she do if their friendship ended? Who would be her support then?

She eased her head up from his shoulder, embarrassed that she'd soiled his shirt with her tears, but his face reflected only sweet kindness. "Thank you, Grif. Your friendship and real concern lifts me up from the darkness that I often feel inside."

"I wish you could let it go, Marcy. Talk about it, and once in the open, the weight could lift off your heart and soul. I know the sadness is deep."

Her chest fluttered as his words saturated her mind. Grif had spoken the truth. She'd heard so often that getting things out in the open was like emptying a closet filled with bad things and tossing them away. Clearing the air. Clearing the body and mind. But how could she?

When she gazed into his eyes, he gave her the

answer. "Marcy, let's sit and maybe you can tell me one thing that's bothering you." His voice filled with question.

A deep desire rose inside her to do what he asked. To spill the filth and hurt from her in the same way her thoughts of emptying the closet had struck her.

She moved back to the sofa and sank into the cushion. Her head spun with her thoughts and his encouragement. What could happen if she opened up to him? What she had to say would be nothing that bad about herself, and maybe just talking about it would do what he said—help lift her from the darkness.

Grif sat beside her, close and yet not too close to crowd her. "Would you like something to drink or—"

"I'm fine." And yet she wasn't. "I've held so much inside me, Grif, that's it's hard to talk about it, and then I ask myself why do you want to spend time with a woman who's so filled with problems?"

"Because I care about her...very much."

She looked into his eyes again, seeing nothing but kindness and concern. That was Grif. She released a lengthy breath. "Okay, first of all, you already know I had a challenging childhood and especially teen years. My parents' marriage was horrible, and I witnessed it. I've told you all of that. The one thing I haven't mentioned was that it is difficult to be an only child with no sibling to talk with."

She turned her eyes to his and seeing his face touched her heart. "I longed to have a brother, because that's what my father wanted and valued. Women were nothing but housekeepers. Remember, 'be seen and not heard.' But I grew up as an only child." She choked on a sob. "And that's where overhearing something has been my curse."

"Please tell me, Marcy. It's the only way you'll be free of the loneliness of carrying the burden."

She'd never thought of it as a burden, but Grif understood and was correct. "One day I overheard my mother on the telephone. What I heard shocked me to the core. I'm not sure who she was talking to, but it was someone who knew the family secret. I spent part of my lifetime wondering if I'd misheard what she'd said, but lately, I'm sure that I hadn't."

"What did you hear, Marcy. Please tell me." Grif pressed his hand against hers. "Let it out."

"My mother mentioned how the grief of giving up her baby daughter for adoption had never left her."

"A daughter? Adoption?" Grif's surprise sounded in his whisper.

"Yes, that's what I heard. And then it all fell into place. I was so young that I hadn't remembered that my mother had gotten pregnant again and when she gave birth to another girl, it made sense, knowing my father, that he would not accept it. He did not want another daughter, so he demanded the child be put up for adoption. My father wanted a boy."

"Oh, Marcy…" Grif moved closer and rested his arm around her shoulders. "And you've been carrying that in your heart all this time without talking about it? Did you ask your mom about—"

"My mother would not speak of it to me. Her face mottled with anger or fear when I asked her. I never knew what emotion, but I knew she wanted me to stop asking. So, I did."

"You'll never know for sure, except for what you heard. Somewhere you have a sister."

"I might, but I'll never know as you said. I've accepted that I am without family, and yet that idea has entered my mind on many occasions, that somewhere I might have family. I might have a sister."

"But you don't have to give up hope, Marcy. Not if you want to give it a try to find out."

"What? Call hospitals or go to county courthouse and try to get birth certificates. I have no idea where to even begin, and would they give me the information anyway?"

"You have one that is easier, but it could be disappointing."

Her pulse skipped seeing the look on his face. "What do you mean?"

"DNA."

"DNA? But I have no idea how that would work."

"Ancestry site offers DNA tests and results. If you have a sibling who was adopted by someone, she might have had a test done to find her parents or other relatives. People want to know about health issues in their birth family and their family history."

What he'd said sank into her thoughts, but it left her confused. "What about the mother and father who raised them. Wouldn't that ruin their relationship or—"

"In most cases, no, Marcy. People usually ask for the approval of their adoptive parents. It's not that they don't have good parents, but they want to know what I said earlier—health issues, historic family history, possible siblings. I knew a family years ago who were thrilled that the son they had adopted found he had a sister. They met and it was a blessing for all of them."

Though what he said made sense, her usual fear grew. Would she waste her time and money to learn no one had her DNA? Or maybe the sister she might find wanted no part of meeting her? Or…

"You look dubious, Marcy. It's only a suggestion. If you want to know bad enough, it's the easiest way to start. DNA tests aren't too expensive and then you have a chance to learn the truth."

"I need to think about it. If someone got in touch with me, would I want to meet the person and—"

"Listen to yourself. You're longing to know if you have a sister. If one contacted you, is there any doubt what you would do? Not in my eyes. You would want to meet her and with open arms. Marcy. Use your head."

She flinched. But immediately faced the truth. Grif had spoken the truth. "You're right. I'm just a coward, Grif. I've hung to this so long that putting it out in the open is as if I'm betraying my mother or betraying my secret."

"Take a breath and see how alleviating speaking out can be. It's no longer a secret. No longer deep inside you. It's on the outside, and you have an action plan to find an answer."

An answer? "You're right, Grif. I have lived in a box for too many years, being seen and not heard…even to myself. I'm like the little mouse hiding from danger, and everything unknown is danger to me. I want to be out in the open. I want out of the box. I want to live my life and not dream about having one."

"And today you're making the first step. Marcy, I'm proud of you. I'm thrilled to hear you say that you want to live, and I'm here to live with you." His arm around her shoulder drew her closer as his eyes searched her face, pausing at her mouth, and lowering his lips to hers."

Longing spread through her body, a sense of wholeness, whether from the possibility of having a sister or admitting she wanted to live. Today, with Grif's loving help, she had opened the door and the windows. She was ready for life to begin.

♥

Spending more time with Marcy had followed the day she'd opened up on her past. Grif had gotten her on horseback again, and this time, he rode beside her on Bandit. Though they walked most of the way, she agreed to take a chance with his instruction to trot. Though a bit edgy, he watched her with pride as she did as he said along with his encouragement. Soon, he hoped, he wouldn't need to persuade her to try new things.

Two weeks passed before he decided to ask Marcy about the DNA. He wanted her to act on getting the test results without his prodding. The outcome of the test could go either way, and the decision had to be Marcy's.

Guiding the last horse into the stable from the corral, he heard the crunch of car tires. When he checked his watch, he assumed Marcy had arrived, and when he stepped into the yard, Marcy smiled as she met him outside the stable door.

"I finally did it." She gazed at him, and from her look, he understood.

"Did you use the Ancestry site?"

She nodded followed by a chuckle. "I had to spit into a little test tube. You know, like the ones in chemistry class. Have you ever had to do that?"

His chuckle joined hers. "Not really, but you never

know. The day may come."

She jostled his arm, sending his heart soaring. Finally, her ability to be playful and comfortable with him had grown into full flower, like a bud that finally bloomed. Her teasing nature branded her the new woman who'd sprouted from the seed of one who needed to be watered and stand in the sunshine.

"How long do you have to wait for results? I suppose it takes a while."

"They said a month or so. But it's something I've waited a lifetime for, so another month or two doesn't upset me."

He slipped his arm around her waist. "Good. It'll give us a gift worth waiting for."

"That's a nice way to look at it." She leaned into him, giving his hip a nudge with hers.

Again, he loved Marcy's progress. "Speaking of gifts, I got the wedding invitation from Betsy. Remember when she said I would be invited. The invitation is to me and a guest. Since I have you cornered here, would you do me the honor of being my date for the wedding?"

She paused and turned to face him. "I wouldn't want it any other way." She leaned toward him and pressed her lips to his. His pulse leaped and his heart soared. Wanting more, he couldn't let her pull away. With his arm still around her waist, he drew her closer, again kissing her as the flames grew, a fire he'd never felt in his life.

When he eased back, Marcy lifted her palm and pressed it on his cheek, her eyes exploring his, a look so tender he could barely contain himself. "Marcy, I have never been happier in my life, and I want you to know that. It's not a line I say to women. It's an admission to you. I thought my life was full with the ranch and the horses, but I now see that it was not even half full, but it is now."

Her gaze stayed connected to his, her cheeks rosy as if the sun had kissed them. "We took two halves, Grif, and made a whole." Misty tears glowed in her eyes. Life had never been as wonderful.

They walked hand in hand into the house, and after he poured them each a soft drink, they settled in the living room on the couch. He enjoyed the sense of togetherness, the slight fresh scent of her fragrance—soap, shampoo or perfume. How would life be if Marcy were with him forever as his wife? She'd been so set against marriage, but she had changed. Could marriage ever be part of her life?

With the thought in his mind, he shifted the conversation back. "By the way, Betsy's wedding is on the last Saturday of October, so that's less than a month away."

"I'll have to buy something to wear, or maybe the dress I had for Ally and Cade's wedding might work. I'll have to think about it."

"No thought on my side. I have the one suit I own." He gave her a wink. "You said I looked good in it."

"No, that's not what I said. I said you looked very handsome."

"You did? Well, that's even better. And I suppose I have to look pretty good, since I'll be escorting the loveliest woman at the affair."

She shook her head, but it didn't need response. Her grin and the color in her cheeks told him she was pleased at what he'd said.

Before he had a chance to talk about dinner, his cell phone rang, and he pulled it from his pocket. He eyed the phone number. "It's Cade." He pushed the button. "Hi, how you doing?"

He listened to Cade, reviewing his suggestion and eyeing Marcy with question. "Just a minute, Cade. I'll check with Marcy." He covered the speaker. "Cade and Ally are inviting us over for a horseback ride and then thought we might like joining them for dinner. What do you say?"

She gazed at him with no reaction, and that threw him. Instead of asking or saying anything, he waited.

"I'm not confident with the riding, but I'm happy about dinner. If we do ride, I'll have to go home and change my clothes."

He nodded. "We'll be over in a while. Probably within the hour. Is that okay?"

Cade said great, so he ended the conversation, and studied Marcy. "I know you're nervous about riding, but it gets dark earlier so I don't think we'll be out long on horseback. So, don't worry. Okay?"

She tilted her head, lifting her shoulder. "I'll manage. But if we're getting there in an hour, I need to get home to change into riding clothes."

He eyed his attire, glad he even had his boots on. "I'm ready. Let's go."

♥

Marcy did the fastest change of clothes she could remember. In jeans, one of her Western shirts and the boots she'd added to her attire, she slipped into Grif's SUV and leaned back, enjoying the blue sky with only a few white, fluffy clouds. The ride from Cottonwood to Sedona took only a half hour unless they ran into an accident or rarely traffic. That was one of the nice things about small town living.

"Do you have preferences for dinner? I'm sure Cade and Ally will ask."

"I'm open to anything. I haven't had Mexican for a while, and I know you like it."

"So does Cade, so let's see."

Though dusk was a few hours off, the sky still held promise of being beautiful. The dark nights in Yavapi County filled the pitch-black sky with a sea of stars and planets. People often sat on their driveways with telescopes, gazing up at the awesome sky. They remained quiet, and sometimes she loved it that way. She and Grif had a solid relationship, it seemed, and speaking every moment had faded into good conversations and time to enjoy the silence.

When he turned on Jack's Canyon Road, she noticed that the sun had lowered but still hung above the red rocks, mesas, buttes, and mountains. The scenery settled in her heart like God's painting.

When they pulled into the ranch, Cade and Ally stood near the stable with four horses saddled and ready to ride. Marcy drew in a breath, again wanting to be strong and agreeable, but still not fully confident in her riding ability. She hoped the others would be patient as Grif was.

Ally and Cade waved as Grif pulled down the ranch driveway and parked between the house and barn. She slipped out to the ground and headed toward Ally with a wave.

"Great to see you." Ally opened her arms wide and Marcy stepped in, realizing how often they didn't see each other since Ally's marriage to Cade. But she understood.

"Good to see you, too." Marcy added a hug.

"Grif tells us you're getting more comfortable on horseback. I'm glad. I remember how often I pushed you to do things you didn't want to do. Now, I understand. You will do them when you are ready. I think I learned a lesson, Marcy."

Marcy only grinned, hoping Ally meant what she said. "I'm not a good rider yet. No speed. Just a trot, but I'll learn to canter soon, I suppose."

"You'll love cantering. It's very comfortable. Not the bouncing that riders often feel. But first the trotting needs to be mastered."

This time Marcy laughed. "Oh yes, bouncing. How could I forget?"

Ally grinned too. "You've made good stride, Marcy. I'm proud of you, and I'm sorry for all my pushing. I realize now that that technique doesn't work. Support and help when asked is what it takes."

"You're right." The change in Ally's attitude had to be influenced by Cade, just as she had learned so much about herself from Grif. Partnerships were very real gifts. When two people support and encourage each other, nothing could be better.

Grif ambled to her side. "Do you need help mounting? By the way, this horse is Belle."

She eyed the stirrup. "I think I can do it myself. Let me try." She slipped her left toe on the broad area of the stirrup and swung her right leg over the horse's back and slipped her right foot in the same spot on the stirrup.

When she turned to Grif, he beamed. "Great job, Marcy. Perfect in fact."

"Thank you. I feel like the 'belle of the ball' right now." Grif's grin grew and she noticed Ally's thumbs up that thrilled her to see her friend's obvious approval.

Marcy slipped the reins lightly in her hand, relaxed her knees against the horse's side and waited until the others were ready. Grif moved alongside her and gave his rein a faint pull. His horse stepped away, and she followed, her chest tight with pride and also with hope that she'd stay on without incident.

The foursome moved at a slow pace over the meadow as the sun lowered toward the horizon. Colors began to appear in the pastel tones of sunset—coral, yellow, gold blending upward to lavender. Though it meant the day's end, the sunset became the happy ever after in a love story. Each day would bring something new and yet end with the soft spread of heavenly creative handiwork.

Cade motioned toward the ranch, and they walked the horse's in a circle and headed back before darkness fell over the meadow. The horse's safety gave high motivation to be back in the stable before dark.

Grif appeared closer beside her. If she reached out, she might be able to touch him, but just knowing he was there gave her total pleasure.

"You did a good job, Marcy. I think Ally's happy too. She wanted the best for you, I'm sure, but didn't know how to go about it."

"She's been forgiven, Grif. She's learned something from it too. I think as I grew stronger, our friendship lessened, and Ally gave that thought. She's apologized for her attempts to push and manipulate, but I'd already forgiven her."

Grif's smile was all she needed to see.

A soft evening breeze brushed through her hair, and before darkness had settled, they reached the ranch and had the horses in the stable. Everyone pitched in as they untacked the horse they road, and after removing the saddle and tack, watering the horse and giving him a brush, they were on their way to dinner.

Grif drove the SUV, and while they headed toward West Sedona, they decided on Mexican food. That made her happy. When they came to the curve on the highway, the Hillside sign faced them and Cade and Grif spoke at the same time. "Javelina Cantina."

They all laughed at the camaraderie. Everyone agreed that's where they would eat. When they arrived, they had a wait, so they settled at a table in the outside setting, and she gazed behind her as one of the shops caught her attention. "How long did they say we had to wait?"

Cade eyed Grif. "I think about twenty minutes to a half hour. We'll order drinks and enjoy the sunset."

"That works well for me." Marcy pointed to the dress shop on the next level. "I think I'll run in there and see what they have. I need a dress for a wedding coming up."

Ally's interest perked. "Whose getting married?"

Marcy almost laughed. She suspected Ally was hoping it was her. "A friend of Grif's, and we're invited."

"Do you mind if I join you?" She pointed to the dress shop.

"Not at all. I'll appreciate your opinion."

While the men ordered drinks, they climbed the stairs and stepped into the boutique. Marcy suspected it might be expensive, but why not try. The clerk greeted them and asked what they were looking for. "A dress for an autumn wedding. I'm just a guest so it doesn't have to be too fancy."

"We have some gowns I think you'll like." The clerk beckoned them to follow.

Marcy gazed at the garments they passed, noting some were too dressy, and trying to glimpse at the price tags, but they were too small. When the clerk stopped in front of display of dresses, she paused and scanned her options. One color popped out from the rest, a lovely medium turquoise with darker delicate scroll-work around the neck and skirt.

She stepped forward and lifted it from the display. "What do you think?" She turned to face Ally.

"It's beautiful, Marcy. The color is perfect for your hair and your blue-green eyes. And I like the line of the dress, form-fitting at the waist and then spilling out into a full a-line. It'll complement your figure. Try it on?"

Marcy eyed her watch. "I'll have to hurry."

The clerk walked her to the dressing room, and she tugged off her clothes and dropped the dress over her head. When she faced the mirror, her pulse skipped. She'd never had a dress that fit so well and complimented her figure as this one did. The delicate scrolling made the neckline pop as well as the flared hem-line. She stepped out of the dressing room and did a full turn. "I love it. Do you agree?"

Ally's smile answered her. "Absolutely perfect."

"I can't believe I found a dress this fast." She darted back into the dressing room, hung the garment on the hanger and slipped on her clothes, as she lifted the dress, her eyes caught the price tag. She gasped as her heart sank. Nice try.

She stepped into the store, shaking her head. "I'll have to keep looking."

"What? It's amazing."

"So is the price." She lifted the tag and showed her.

"But that's not bad, Marcy. It's a beautiful dress and you look amazing in it. Once in a while we deserve something special. You work hard for your pay, I know, and this dress was meant for you."

Still gaping at the price tag, she let it fall from her hand but continued to gaze at the dress. Ally made sense. For once, she could treat herself to something special She'd never done that before.

She grinned at Ally. "You're right."

Ally glowed as they walked to the checkout counter. "Can I leave the dress here until after dinner?"

"Certainly. I'll tag the bag for you."

"Thanks so much." She pulled out her credit card, watched the clerk ring it up and then signed the receipt.

The clerk slipped her a copy and attached another copy to the bag. "Don't worry about the dress. It will be here when you come back."

Ally took her arm and tilted her head toward the door. "I think they're being called in. I saw Cade looking this way."

"Perfect dress and perfect timing." Marcy's spirit sang as they exited and followed the men into Javelina Cantina.

Chapter 7

Curious, Grif headed for Marcy's front door, anxious to see the dress she'd bought at the Hillside shop. She'd stopped to collect it after they'd enjoyed their tasty Mexican meal at Javelina Cantina. He always got a kick out of the interesting log that hung over the cantina's fireplace, shaped as a Javelina's head. The art work intrigued him.

He'd only seen a live Javelina once when hiking through a Sedona wooded area. He had no idea of their size, appearing to be a large boar, and yet a Javelina was a peccary and not from the pig family. It probably was the uniqueness that caught everyone's interest in the wild Southwest animal.

When he reached the porch, his mind left the topic and fell back to what he awaited, seeing Marcy in her new dress. He lifted his finger to ring her doorbell, and before he touched it, she opened the door. He stumbled back, his breath escaping him. She looked gorgeous.

"Marcy, you look...out of this world. The color..." He faltered, hearing his attempt to compliment her without the right words.

"Thank you, Grif." A faint grin settled on her face and she pushed open the door. "Would you like to come in, or are you ready to go?"

"I'm ready when you are."

"Wait one minute. I'll grab something in case it's cool this evening." She turned and appeared a moment later.

When she stepped outside, he took her arm and waited for her to settle into the passenger seat before rounding the car. Once in the driver's seat, he turned to face her. "You look amazing, Marcy. You take my breath away."

She shook her head and grinned. "Thank you, again. I questioned myself paying so much for the dress, but I decided to give myself a gift, and this is it. Hearing you say you think it's lovely validates the expense."

"You never need validation, Marcy. You deserve so much more than you give yourself. In my eyes, you'll be the belle of the ball." He chuckled at the old phrase and started the car.

Grif followed the highway toward uptown, and when he spotted the well-known Tlaquepaque Spanish-style Arch, he pulled into the parking lot. "Now to find the chapel."

He rounded the car and opened the door for Marcy, and for once she'd remained seated so he could be a gentleman. When she stepped out, again, her appearance rocked his usual steady frame. A breath escaped him, and he grinned at her and shrugged. "I think you've about knocked me off my feet."

"You're a handsome man yourself, Grif. You just don't believe me."

He wanted to, but his world had always been jeans and boots. He linked his arm with hers and headed into the arts and crafts village with its stucco walls covered in vines and tile or cobblestone pathways. In a matter of minutes, he spotted the steeple of what appeared to be a Spanish Chapel, a large concrete cross stood in front, carved with an attractive scrolled pattern from the past.

They were greeted at the door by one of the groomsmen, and when they walked in, Marcy faltered, a soft wow slipping from her lips. "This is gorgeous."

Ahead of them, a huge gold frame housed a religious piece of artwork, and the pastel walls emphasized the beauty. A long mahogany credenza stretched along the wall beneath the painting holding two large floral arrangements. He chose to sit further back on the bride's side of the room to leave seating for Betsy's family and close friends towards the front.

The soft music grew as the guests hushed, signaling the beginning of the wedding. He studied the affair, trying to picture himself as the groom. The new thought unsettled him, but didn't surprise him since he'd fallen in love with Marcy. He'd said nothing to her, but he could no longer hide it from himself.

Every step of the wedding, he noted what was done and what was said, and when he had a chance, he gave a subtle glance at Marcy who appeared to be caught up in the beauty of the service. But she surprised him following the sharing of rings, when she gazed at him with an amazing smile. "This is lovely, Grif."

She was lovely. But he couldn't tell her that now. Instead, he nodded in agreement.

They rose when the bride and groom turned toward their guests before making their way down the aisle to the back of the church. Once there, the couple would be greeted and congratulated. But he and Marcy didn't hurry. Instead he again studied the beautiful venue and considered if he would want a wedding here or…

Weddings? Marriage? All new ideas that now punctured his quiet moments with longing. He'd lived alone for his adult life, but not long ago, he faced a truth. A legacy meant leaving something of value to others. He had no others to leave anything to—not family, a wife or a child, and in a few more years, he would be too old to raise a child.

When the chapel emptied except for a final few, he grasped Marcy's hand and led her outside where they greeted Betsy and her new husband, Craig. He gave Betsy a hug and shook hands with Craig. Grif's chest swelled, when Betsy greeted Marcy by name as she admired Marcy's dress.

As they left the greeting line, he spotted the other guests heading toward a row of trees rising along Oak Creek, and he noticed a large flagstone patio beneath the trees. "That looks like the reception area." He pointed to the tables covering the expanse.

"The setting is lovely. It looks like nature with the beige cloths and napkins, the white china, and a white floral plant with spring green leaves. They didn't miss a thing."

"And neither did you." He grinned at her elaborate description, one worth looking at. "Let's find our seats. I'm guessing they're marked in some way."

When they stepped onto the flagstone and approached the tables, he'd been right. "Look for our name tags by the plates."

Marcy walked ahead of him, checking the name plates, and soon, she beckoned him and pointed to the two sets close to the rippling water. He held the chair for her, and when she was seated, he slipped into the one next to her. As guests came, he only recognized a few people who were related to Betsy, but even the strangers were friendly.

Trays of appetizers where passed by the servers, and drinks were available nearby, but he and Marcy didn't need to stand since they both enjoyed their glasses of iced water. Once Betsy and Craig settled at the head table with their attendants, the main course was served with choices of chicken or beef dishes and a variety of sides.

As the sun lowered in the sky, stringed lights came on around the patio, creating a romantic aura for the special occasion. A small band who'd played soft dinner music, now added volume to encourage guests to dance. Though not a dancer, he'd realized at Cade and Ally's wedding that he knew enough to enjoy the moment of holding Marcy in his arms.

A love song filled the air, and he reached for Marcy's hand, and she rose, joining him on the dance floor. Again, the touch of her body against his, the feel of her soft cheek and hand, riled his emotions as his pulse tripped along his arms. His knees seemed to lose their strength, and he yearned to tell Marcy how he felt, but he feared her reaction. Would she withdraw and vanish from his life? Would she grow distant and refuse spending time with him? Would she say she felt the same?

If he never spoke, he would never know, but taking the chance weighed heavily on his heart. He cared too much to plow right in. The wait needed consideration— to tiptoe or offer one small hint after another until his feelings were in the open. But could he take time to do that?

As they continued into the next love song, Marcy leaned her head on his shoulder, her body pressing against this chest, and he guessed she could feel the beating of his heart. To him, it pumped and pounded.

The ease of her body, moving with him in rhythm, swinging out and in without a stumble, the joy of sharing the moment, etched in his brain, and he could imagine life with Marcy in quiet conversation, romantic kisses, and sometimes laughing at their foolishness. Yes, they would have disagreements, but they'd talked through many misunderstandings since they'd met. She'd been so careful and edgy at first, but then time passed, and their relationship grew.

Marcy tilted her head upward, her eyes searching his. "Thank you for bringing me here, Grif. It was a lovely wedding, and now it's a beautiful reception. The venue is perfect, as I said, like being surrounded by nature and the amazing creation of Sedona."

"And sunset adds to the setting, don't you think?" He brushed her cheek with his fingers, and then twirled her to the beat of the music.

"Sunset is putting a star-like period on the end of a tremendous experience. I agree."

He pictured the evening sky growing faster as the sun vanished, the billions of tiny sparkles in the blackness, hanging there like the lights that brightened the wedding guests around the flagstone.

"Marcy, I'm so happy to be sharing this night with you. I love that you see the night as I do. Not something frightening, but a reminder that the day will sleep and be awakened in the morning to give us another bright day. I want to have many days with you, Marcy. I hope—"

"I feel the same, Grif. I've fought my feelings during my lifetime, knowing that I don't deserve them or am fooling myself, but not since I've met you. I want more days, days like this one, filled with love around us, natural beauty, special music and quality time together."

He took a chance and lowered his lips to hers. She eased closer, her mouth moving with his, her breath coming in gasps, her body trembling with anticipation, and he sent up a thank you to the Lord for giving him an opportunity to live a full life—not as a loner but as a man who shares his hours, months and years, with the special woman in his life.

♥

Marcy trudged in from work, aware that the wedding and working the next day had been a poor plan, but sometimes she had no choice. She'd danced the night away, relishing in the feel of being in Grif's arms, his tender words, and her ability to open up, added to the new Marcy. She'd begun to love herself, and it dawned on her if she didn't love herself no one else would either.

She dropped her handbag on the nearest table and sank into her recliner. Drawing in a deep breath, she let her shoes drop to the ground and wiggled her toes. She pushed the recline-handle and her legs bounced up leaving her in a great position for a nap. But she really didn't have time for a meaningful rest since she'd left many things undone that needed doing.

She lowered her legs and bent down to pick up her shoes before she rose. Heading into the bedroom to change clothes, she passed her computer and paused. The DNA results would be arriving soon and her curiosity rose.

She set her shoes on the floor, pulled out a chair, and started her computer to check her email. Her heart skipped when she spotted what she'd waited for. She clicked on the link and stared at the DNA results.

She scanned the message as her pulse hammered in her temples. The connection she saw was a female, a possible sister. The name filled her mind—Lacy Jordan. An email link sat nearby, and she closed her eyes struggling with what she wanted to do. Talk with Grif arose first in her thoughts. He would help her deal with the situation.

The computer could sit there a few minutes, while she rose and hurried to the bedroom to change into more comfortable clothes. She sat on the edge of her bed and punched in Grif's phone number. It rang while she tapped her heel as she waited.

She heard a blip and expected to hear a recording, but instead, Grif's greeting met her ears. "Hi, Marcy. I bet your tired today."

"I am, but that's not why I called. Guess what?" She sat a moment wishing she wouldn't have posed the question instead of just telling him.

"You won a million dollars?"

"That was a rotten guess to answer a bad question. My DNA results are in."

"Wow, Marcy. What news did you get?"

"That's why I'm calling. I'm not sure what I want to do. I have a possible sister, and I have an email address, but contacting her right now might not be a good move."

"What's your concern? This is what you've been waiting for."

"I know, Grif, but she may not have checked her email. She might not be prepared and does she want to talk with me? I'm trying to put my feet in her shoes."

"Marcy, look at it this way. If she hadn't wanted to learn about family, she wouldn't have had a DNA test done. Doesn't that make sense?"

"I suppose it does, but—"

"I do understand the first thing you said. She may not have read her email yet. I don't know if that makes a difference, but you could wait a day or so, and see if she contacts you. You'd be ready for it."

"I would be...very ready. The site says she is probably a sister, so I assume that it would say the same on her test results too. Right?"

"Absolutely. If you can bear to wait a day, you might feel better about the contact, but if you can't wait, then wait until this evening and call. Right now, all you've done is to send an email. Do you know where she lives?"

She shook her head and then laughed at herself. "No, only an email address, and so waiting does make sense. Time zones vary and it might be later in the day. She might be at work or..."

"I'd be happy to come over when you call, Marcy, if you think you'll need support. I doubt it though. My guess is that she's as anxious as you are."

"You're probably right. Her name gave me a moment of thought."

"In what way?"

"It's similar to mine. If my mom named her and they kept the name, it makes sense or it could be a coincidence, I suppose."

"Now that we've covered that, give me a hint.

What's her name?"

"Lacy."

"Marcy. Lacy. I can see why you considered the name might have been given her by your mom. Interesting."

"But then I could be totally wrong."

He chuckled but didn't say a word.

"Okay, you've convinced me. I'll wait until tomorrow and see if she calls me first. Otherwise—"

"You'll call her. Good plan, and hey, if you want to come over tonight, I'd love to see you. We could—"

"I have lots to do, and I'm really tired, Grif. I'll see you tomorrow. Maybe I could have another horseback lesson."

"That made me smile, Marcy. Hope you have a good evening and call me if you hear anything before tomorrow."

"I will. Goodnight, Grif."

"Good night, my sweet one."

His endearment rippled through her chest and warmed her heart. Grif had given her a new life, new longings, and new experiences. The awareness made her grin. She begun to sound like Ally who'd spent a huge hunk of her life looking for fun, adventure and excitement. Unlike Ally, without spending her life searching, she'd found all three experiences and all with one man—Griffin Coleman, her treasure.

♥

Grif hadn't heard a word from Marcy, and his curiosity piled in his thoughts until he could barely remember his daily tasks. He'd forgotten to put the horses in the corral until dusk had already fallen. His mistake cheated the horses on their time for exercise and fresh air. Getting himself under control had become his priority.

Though he could call Marcy, for some reason, he sensed this big life change for her needed to be private—at least, until she was ready to talk with him. He suspected the sister had not contacted her...and the same with Marcy. He figured she hadn't made contact either. Why? His only guess could be fear of disappointment.

He'd picked up his cell phone numerous times and then put it away. And facing a new day, he considered putting his phone in a drawer and leaving it there until he took care of his ranch tasks, especially the horses. He hadn't ridden any of the horses since the last time he went out with Marcy.

Fighting his longing to call her, he won the battle, He slipped on his boots and headed toward the stable. When he stepped inside, he stopped to greet each horse with a treat, their favorite—an apple. While they chomped, he lifted Lady's saddle and set it aside until he took the others out to the corral.

One by one, he led the horses into the enclosure where they had water, some hay and a place to move about. Then he returned to the stable and saddle up Lady. When he settled on her back, he steered her toward the stable door. Outside he signaled her to walk, and he headed to the meadow, knowing that the exercise would be short but at least, she would have a chance to trot.

When he signaled her forward, she gained momentum, and facing his lack of attention to the horses caused him to grimace at his distraction. Marcy meant the world to him, but his horses were his life.

They deserved his time and love.

Lady headed into the meadow with a new spirit, and so did he. Riding always gave him pleasure, and he'd been missing the freedom of cantering across the broad open fields, enjoying the landscape of red rocks, buttes, mesas and mountains. The fresh air ruffled his hair and the sun warmed his arms. Since he'd met Marcy, his life had changed in some good ways and some not so good.

With his eye on the time, he rounded Lady back toward the ranch, hoping he might have time to take another horse out later in the day. With the plan in his head, he galloped back to the ranch and faltered when he saw Marcy's car parked near the barn. His chest tightened, trying to ready himself for what was to come—her disappointment or her happiness.

She waved as he rode closer, and she followed behind Lady as they road to the stable. When he dismounted, she stood nearby, waiting for him to take care of Lady first. But his curiosity got the better of him. "Are you alright?"

She nodded with no hint of emotion, and her strange response caused his uneasiness.

When he removed the tack, he led Lady to the water trough, and while she drank, he brushed her, though his mind clung to Marcy's expression. Finished, he placed an apple in his palm, and Lady took it and settled into her stall.

"The horses need more exercise. I've been lax on keeping up with their needs." After saying what he did, he imagined Marcy blaming herself. "It's my neglect, Marcy. Please don't—"

"That was the old Marcy, Grif. I understand. The

horses are your job, just as the hospital work is mine. We allow things to distract us, and it's our fault alone."

A ragged breath seeped from his lungs. "That's correct." He moved closer to her and grasped her hand. "We need to ride more, I'm thinking. You're experienced enough to trot out with me in the meadow and help exercise the horses while we have time to talk and enjoy being in nature."

"You're right. It's a good experience for me too."

He loved hearing her be positive. "Have you heard anything?"

"No, but I've decided to give it time. She might be on vacation or have someone ill in the family or a number of other things. Not everyone opens their computer every day."

"Me, for one. I don't look as often as I should since that's part of my business." He shrugged. "I need an assistant." He gave her a toying smile.

"Have you interviewed yet?" She grinned back, obviously catching on to his innuendo.

"Now, you're telling me you don't want the job."

She squeezed his hand. "I didn't say that, but then I'd be working two jobs and I'd have no time for—"

"Maybe one of these days, you won't need the other job...unless you love it so much you wouldn't want to quit."

"Not so much, but I do like to eat and pay my bills."

He lifted a shoulder. "Things can happen, you know."

She pressed her lips together, her eye lids nearly closed, and he longed to know her thoughts, but what she might have on her mind caused him concern. His chest tightened as he studied her face. She'd looked out across the meadow and he had no idea what ideas or plans had settled in her mind…or if he were part of those plans.

When she looked his way, her eyes met his. "I'm off tomorrow so I'll come over early and help with the horses. Is that okay?"

"Okay?" He eased closer to her. "I'm content and happy when you're with me, Marcy. I love being with you whether we're working, riding horses or plain old sitting in a chair talking."

"Me, too, Grif. But when I know you have work, then helping you makes me happy."

He could contain himself no longer. He slipped his free arm around her and drew her closer. As she stood in his arms, her head resting on his shoulder, he envisioned life with her today and when they grew old and gray. He prayed she shared his thoughts.

Taking a chance, he tilted her chin upward, searched her eyes, and then lowered his lips to meet hers. Her giving kiss assured him of her feelings, and now what he had to do was test reality. He loved her. He'd answered that question, and seeing her in his dreams for a lifetime validated his desire to ask her to be his wife. All he needed now was the courage.

Marcy's phone rang cancelling his wandering thoughts. He dropped his arms, and she dug into her pocket and pulled out the phone. "It's Ally." She answered, then looked at him and grinned. "Cade's been trying to call you. Ally thought I might know where you are." She arched an eyebrow. "And I do." She handed him her phone.

Grif stared at the phone a moment before putting it to his ear. "Ally, I'm home, but my cell phone is in the house. Do you need me for something?"

He listened and cringed when he heard her question. "How long did you say? Three hours. Hang on a minute."

A frown rose on Marcy's face. "What is it?" Her eyes searched his.,

"They're going out with friends and their babysitter backed out on them at the last minute, so they wondered if I could keep an eye of the girls for three hours." He studied her expression that had now become a grin. He shrugged not thinking it was funny. "Can you stick around?"

Her grin broadened. "I think I can manage it."

Relief washed over him, and his heart filled with Marcy's kindness. "Thanks." He pulled the phone back to his ear. "I can do that, Ally. Marcy dropped by, and she said she'd stick around to help entertain the girls."

Ally gushed her gratitude with tons of thank yous, and he kept his voice calm while his plans faded. He'd have to find another time to have the serious conversation with Marcy about their future.

That is if he could find the courage that he'd hoped to exhibit this day. A breath rattled from his lungs. At least with the delay, he had time to work on it.

Chapter 8

The twins proved to be easier to watch than Marcy expected. She took them outside to feed the horses and then led them to the corral which gave Grif time to run to his store, Western Outlet, and check on a few things. After she'd tried everything she could think of, she recalled their love of puzzles. Now to find where Grif had put them.

She looked in the most logical places and then stared around the rooms eyeing the most improbable places. Her last effort was the linens closet where she found success. She had to hold her side that ached from laughing so hard.

The twins settled at the table, spreading the pieces out and separating the edges from the middle pieces. She stood over them for a few minutes, and when she knew they were committed to the activity, she wandered away and settled in Grif's recliner, lifting the footrest. Her body relaxed as she listened to the girls, laughing and discussing which puzzle piece went where. She gazed around the room with its masculine décor and yet it seemed appropriate for a horse ranch.

Her gaze landed on a pile of magazines sitting in a rack, and her attention caught one that appeared to be

Western décor and even clothing. With her curiosity rising, she picked up the slippery paged catalog and flipped through the pages. The more she looked, the more ideas she had for Grif's store in town.

Though Grif had standard Western attire and tack for horses, her interest had been drawn to numerous other items—baby clothes featuring ponies, children's western T-shirts with frolicking horse images, and picture books. Even jewelry, something she rarely wore, caught her eye. She hoped Grif would like her ideas.

She rose and spotted a pencil and pad of paper in the kitchen, and when she returned, she jotted down catalog pages with a brief description. She would love to manage a place like that, especially if the job were only from nine to six. When she leaned back again, second thoughts spiraled in her head. Grif might not like her interference. Still, he might. He mentioned needing an assistant. Images rose in her mind as she considered if she'd like her work at the shop.

Definitely.

Laughter reached her, and she dropped the footrest and headed to the girls, hoping the laughter was to do with the puzzle and nothing else. When she arrived, she saw the problem. "Someone got mixed up, I think." She pointed to a section with no pieces and too many puzzle parts popping up out of another section. "You can't force them in girls. They should drop in without a wrestling match."

They covered their mouths as giggles spilled out from behind their hands.

Marcy settled in a chair nearby and pointed. "Okay, let's pull out those pieces and start again."

Chloe grinned and pointed to Jolie. "I told her that wasn't where they went."

"But you forced them in anyway." Jolie glared at Chloe her hand on her hip.

Marcy reached out and patted the puzzle. "No blaming each other. We all make mistakes, especially on jigsaw puzzles. So instead of blaming, let's fix it."

The two girls eyed each other, giggled again and settled back into the chairs. She didn't want to interfere, so she watched them while trying to keep her mouth shut. Ready to burst, she couldn't hold herself back. "Let's take a look at that puzzle piece. What do you see?"

Chloe mentioned seeing the corner of the saddle while Jolie referred to the puzzle shape. "It's a saddle, Chloe, but see on the puzzle cover, there are two horses, so maybe this piece goes with the other horse." Chloe studied the puzzle picture on the lid, and when she looked up, she grinned. "You're right."

Marcy loved seeing the girls get along so well, even when they sometimes disagreed. She rose ready to move back to the recliner when an awareness made her pause. So often, even though marriage had been out of the picture, she'd considered herself lacking in motherly instincts, and yet she'd child-sat the twins a number of times, and she'd done a good job.

Instead of leaving, she studied the two young faces, curious what her own daughter or son might look like. The question had tumbled through her mind and surprised her. Marriage had been a no-no, so having a child would end the consideration of what her child would look like, what personality would he or she have, and what talents. She had few.

Her mind juggling a multitude of ideas and questions, she jerked to a stop when she heard the door open. She stepped toward the living room as Grif headed toward her. "How did it go?"

"Great." She told him about working with the horses and finding the puzzle in his linen closet. The image of the puzzle boxes piled next to the towels and sheets caused her to laugh again.

"Hey, men have a different style of organization."

"I guess so. I'd like to see where you keep your toothbrush."

He slipped his arm around her waist and chuckled with her.

While the girls were involved with the puzzle, she tilted her head toward the living room with the plan to talk with him about her additions to his store. But once they slipped onto the couch, she lost her courage. "How were things at the store?"

"Fine. With school beginning now, the tourists will slow down, but the shop still gets a lot of local trade, so I'm happy. I put in an order for a few things that we needed."

As he talked about merchandise, her courage awoke. "Speaking of that…" She rose and picked up the catalog and settled beside him. "I noticed this catalogue and had some interesting ideas. Do you mind?"

A frown slipped over his face but faded when he tilted his head as if trying to figure out what she meant. "Mind what?"

"I saw some products in the catalogue that I thought would bring in more business, and in the same vein, would be appreciated by your customers since, I think, it's unique and will appeal to women who are probably not your biggest customers."

He studied her a moment, and then nodded. "Right. Most of them are men, but then men are usually the ones who do most of the ranching."

"But the new products would be a drawing point for females. I'm sure."

"Okay, now that you've captured my attention, tell me what you're talking about."

"Now, don't laugh, and let me explain." She began with the children's Western clothes, followed by the jewelry and other items that she would like. "And if you want to check on the kids' attitude, we can ask Chloe and Jolie."

Before she could move, the girls darted into the room and stood there staring at them. "You talked about us." Chloe frowned as if she had blamed the child for doing something bad.

"I did mention you. I thought you could tell me what you think of my idea."

Their expressions changed to grins, and they hurried forward, looking around as if they expected to see bags full of goodies.

"Look at these T-shirts with the horses almost dancing, and see they come in pink, blue and other colors. What do you think of them?"

Jolie's eyes brightened. "Ahh, they're cute." She looked at Chloe. "We have horses, so I like them. Do you Chloe?"

Chloe eyed the catalog for a moment. "I like them too, but look at the baby clothes. I wish I had them." She let out a squeal. "Jolie, look at this T-shirt. It has all the pretty colors and the horse is sparkly."

Grif leaned over and eyed the catalog. "I'd hate for someone to come here and want to ride a sparkly horse."

The twins giggled and laughed until, Marcy had to quiet them. "Okay, girls. Thanks, and you can go back to that puzzle before your daddy comes to get you." She checked her watch, surprised how the time had flown.

Babbling about the sequin-covered horse, they returned to the dining room table and settled in front of the puzzle, their giggles still coming through the doorway.

"Now we know how to entertain the kids." She grinned at Grif.

"Marcy, you are a talent, and I'll tell you what..." His eyes shifted to the catalog. "I'll give your idea some thought. In fact, I'm friendly with a couple of other shop owners in the area, and I'll get their opinion. Adding what you suggested won't cut into their inventory."

He walked behind her and rested a hand on each of her shoulders. "You might have a good idea. It's interesting, and we could start small and then add if it brings in more customers."

"Right, and getting opinions makes sense." His comment hung in her mind until she couldn't contain herself. "And what do you mean...we could start small? Who's the we?"

He leaned over her and bent down to kiss her cheek. "My new assistant."

"And who might that be?" Her heart skipped as the question left her.

"I'll have to see, but I think someone has already volunteered. She's a wonderful woman, very creative and thoughtful. The kind of person that I enjoy spending time with."

"I like people who are thoughtful and kind, too." A flutter swept up her arm. "And I adore people who help me make wise decisions, Grif. Today I did a lot of thinking, and it dawned on me that I'm not bad with children. I've had good experiences with the twins..." She eyed the archway and lowered her voice "I told you what we did today, and I surprised myself. It's sort of fun to realize that you're not the person you always thought you were. Instead you're someone who hid until the right situations encouraged you to leave your hideout. You did that for me, Grif."

"And you've done more than you'll know for me, Marcy." He paused, his gaze shifting to the doorway and then back to her. "We need to talk. Soon."

His tender words touched her to the core, but the word, soon, made her wonder. And yet it also made her think. If she didn't make contact with Lacy, she may never open the door for another new step in her life. Meeting a sister.

♥

Grif stood in the store, eyeing the layout. If he moved the horse tack to the side wall, it would open a place closer to the door for Marcy's idea of adding some Western-themed T-shirts and other paraphernalia. The more he'd considered the idea, the more he liked it. Marcy had added so much to his life and now, she even contributed to his business.

The bell jingled on the door, and he turned, faltering when he saw his customer. "Cade, good to see you. What are you doing in Cottonwood?"

A silly grin stole over Cade's face. "Why? Is there a

rule I can't shop in Cottonwood?"

"No. In fact, I'm glad you dropped by." He extended his hand, and Cade gripped it and gave him a shoulder shake with the other hand.

"Ally wanted to do some shopping in town, so I dropped her off and said I'd stop over here to see you. She'll text me when she's ready."

"You couldn't have come here at a better time. I'm trying to envision a new layout for the store." Grif explained his idea while Cade listened, but in the back of Grif's mind, he had some other concerns as well.

"What made you come up with that idea?"

Grif paused, seeing the odd expression on Cade's face.

"Why, does it sound stupid?"

"No, it's a great idea. We get tons of tourists in this area as well as people who love the West. Why not offer a practical souvenir like a T-shirt or piece of Western jewelry?"

Air escaped his lungs allowing him to relax his tense shoulders. "I'm glad you said that. You had me wondering for a minute."

Cade shook his head. "Don't be edgy, Grif. It's a good idea. I'm guessing you didn't come up with the idea alone. Am I right?"

"It was Marcy. She found some kind of horse focused catalog and suggested it. I agreed it was worth a try."

"And it is." Cade gave him a thumbs up. "It's a good idea to move the saddles and other tack toward the back since that's the store's main seller, but when they walk in, the first thing they'll see is the new stock you've added. Kids will love T-shirts with horses, and

I'm guessing women will too if they're subtle and attractive."

"Thanks for the validation. For some reason, I'm becoming a little shaky with decisions and how to go about them."

Cade eyed him a moment while Grif squirmed beneath his scrutiny.

"Yes, Cade. It's not just the store, its…"

"Marcy." Cade dropped his hand on Grif's shoulder. "Have you told Marcy how you feel?"

Grif looked away, the usual "should haves" and "need tos" filling his mind. "It's a long story, Cade. I'm so confused." He brushed hair from his forehead. "My feelings for her deepen every day, and I've told her that we needed to talk." A rugged blast of air shot from his lungs.

"Then talk with her. She's probably waiting since you told her that you need to talk."

"But-but when I told her, I saw concern in her eyes, and if she tells me that she doesn't feel the same, it'll break me in pieces. I've never opened myself to anyone like that. Not a soul."

Cade gave Grif's shoulder a pat and dropped his hand. "Listen, I don't have all the answers, but I've seen the two of you together, and I can't imagine Marcy telling you to get out of her life. She might be nervous about making a commitment, but letting her know that you care that much for her should at least open the door to testing the water. You know what I mean."

Grif nodded. He understood but concern permeated his mind so deep it left him confused. But he had to trust himself and what God had in store for him.

"You're right, Cade. I'll never know anything if I

don't step out and act, but I'm wondering about the timing. Did you know about Marcy's DNA test?"

Cade's head jerked upward. "Ally mentioned something about Marcy's possibly having a relative that she didn't know about."

"Right. But it's a sister. Apparently, her mother gave her second child for adoption. It's a long story, but Marcy had an idea that something had happened and that's when she decided to do the DNA test. With that filling her head, I'll hold back with my declaration of feelings. Love, if I'm honest. Marcy's mind is filled with the possibility of a sister and I don't want to avert her attempt to deal with that information now. My feelings can come when she knows if she has a sister or not. That's all she's talked about since the DNA results."

"Maybe you're right, but don't put it off any longer than you have to. That's just my opinion."

"Thanks, Cade. You've made the big step into marriage, and I know you're happy so I value your opinion. I've been alone a long time, and I look forward to the day when I have someone who loves me, willing to make a commitment."

"Marcy will. I'm sure, Grif. Very sure."

Grif managed a grin, but he wished he had as much confidence as Cade had.

♥

Marcy couldn't get the hope of having a sister out of her mind. Waiting for a call became a downer, and now she questioned if making the call herself might be fruitless. She didn't need another rejection in her life and calling meant taking a chance.

Though she focused on her job as much as possible,

Grif's hint that she could be working for him kept slipping into her head with a big question mark. Did he mean it? The more she weighed the answer, the more she faced that working for him might be all he had on his mind. He'd been sweet and romantic, enticing her to be an employee. Nothing more.

With too much stressing her mind, she pushed herself through the day, unable to be decisive about anything. At the end of the day, Ally caught up with her in the parking lot, and she stood in front of her mute.

"What's wrong? You look upset or confused. Something's bothering you."

"Yes, something. I don't know what it is, Ally. I'm going in circles." As they stood together as workers passed them heading for their cars, she tried to explain her concerns. "I don't know what I think anymore, Ally. I'm struggling with a possible sister and wrestling with Grif's attempts at making me feel cared about…loved, I don't know."

Ally slipped her arm around her shoulders. "How did you get so messed up, Marcy? You know that Grif has feelings for you. Big feelings as far as Cade and I see. Why are you doubting him now?"

Tears blurred her eyes as a jagged breath rattled from her lungs. "I don't know. I question people's sincerity lately. I'm worthless trying to forget my upbringing that left me feeling worthless, and yet it keeps jabbing me, laughing at me. Why would anyone care about me, let alone love me, Ally? It makes no sense."

"Dear Lord, Marcy, and I mean that. The Lord created you in his image. You have His gifts and some of His attributes. Why would you be lesser than others?

We are all a gift from God. You know your father had severe problems. His hatred chopped any goodness into bits and pieces and left all of you wounded. Have you heard from Lacy?"

"No. Maybe that's what's bothering me."

"Had you thought that she might be home crying, because her older sister is rejecting her. Have you even pictured that? It's not a contest who calls who first. One of you have to show courage and make the call."

Ally's comments ping-ponged from one side of her head to the other. "I suppose you're right."

"Suppose? I am right, and either you need to act or walk away and give up. Which sounds more intelligent?"

"Don't ask me stupid questions, and you're pushing me again."

"Marcy, I'm not pushing. I'm trying to help you see that, for some reason, you're slipping back into the old Marcy who did nothing and said little. You don't deserve to be that person who was damaged. Be the new person that you found hiding inside you. Be strong. Be bold. Take a chance, and it's not really a chance. Someone responded to you who is most likely your sister, the only relative you have. Open the door, Marcy. Let her into your life."

Her tears turned from a trickle on her cheek to a deep sob. Ally knew her and reminded her of how far she'd come until she got back on the slide and landed on her butt in the mud again. While Ally's face showed her sadness, Marcy drew on her strength. "You're right. Absolutely right. I'm drifting away on a paper raft, Ally. I need to get off the raft and swim to shore."

Ally gave her a hug. "Let me know how the call

goes, Marcy. I'm so anxious to hear more about your sister, and don't forget about Grif. He cares more than you know."

♥

"Something's wrong." Grif jerked his head, hearing himself speak out loud. He'd tried to contact Marcy more than once and sensed she'd put up large barriers in her avoidance to talk with him. He'd longed to open his heart, but she'd closed the door.

Needing someone to talk with, he jumped into the SUV and turned onto Cornville Road heading for the Village of Oak Creek where Cade lived. As he drove, he searched for words to explain his feelings and his fears. Men often kept their problems to themselves, but he had to talk with someone and having no family, Cade came the closest.

As the red rocks came into sight, his chest heaved as he still struggled with what to say and how to say it. When he turned onto Jack's Canyon road, he slowed while he questioned turning around and wrestling with his own problems.

Courage. He drew up his shoulders and stepped on the gas, rolling up the incline and making the turn along Lee Mountain. The ranch came into sight, and he sensed Cade's car would be nowhere in sight, which would cause him to do what he'd considered—turn around and go back. But when he spotted not only Cade's car, but Cade working with a horse near the stable, he caught his breath.

He pulled down the driveway, happy to see that Cade gave him a wave as he pulled up to park.

"This is a nice surprise, Grif? Good to see you."

Grif winced inside too aware of his reason for

showing up. "Thanks. I was passing and… Listen, I might as well admit that I needed someone to talk with, and you're the first one that came to mind."

A faint frown flashed on Cade's face before he offered a friendly nod. "I hope I can help, Grif."

He wasn't sure anyone could help. The problem had grown with even more complexities. "I suppose you can guess what this is regarding."

Cade drew back, his eyebrow arching. "Did I do—"

"Heck, no, Cade. You've been a great friend. It's the usual problem men have when falling for a woman."

A grin grew on Cade's face. "Sorry, I don't mean to smile, but you're right. As much as Ally and I loved each other, we had problems too. What's up with you and Marcy? Although Ally and I both noticed she's preoccupied with—"

"Right, that mysterious sister. I've encouraged her to write her again, and she's determined to wait for Lacy's response, which means, Marcy's off in her own world again, feeling snubbed and not worthy and… Cade, it's breaking my heart." Grif bit his lip, tossing admissions in his head that he wasn't sure he wanted to say out loud, but then that's what he'd come for.

Cade nodded. "I'm sure the idea of having family fills her mind, but not getting any contact doesn't mean the sister isn't interested. There are many reasons why she hasn't contacted her. Maybe she hasn't seen Marcy's response. Maybe she's on vacation or staying with someone who is ill, or her computer isn't working or—"

"I tried to tell her that, but Marcy has spent so much of her life feeling worthless that she's slipped back into that person again. Cade, it's tearing me to bits. I…"

Cade grasped his shoulder and shook his head. "All you can do is support her, Grif. Let her know you care about her…love her, I'm sure, and…"

"Here's the meat of the situation. I do love Marcy, and I had planned to ask her to marry me. I'd been working up the courage, fearing exactly what she fears—that someone will say I don't love you, or just a plain no."

Cade gave his shoulder a shake. "Listen, you have taken a long time to contemplate marriage, and I know you'll be an amazing husband. You and Marcy will make a loving couple and great parents. I have no doubt. Right now, maybe, you'll have to support Marcy with the sister situation, and hang on to your feelings until you have her full attention."

"I know. That's what I've realized, and it makes me upset. I should have done it a while ago, but here I am a grown man, a man who's lived alone all these years, who didn't think he needed anyone, and now I let the chance pass me by because I was gutless."

"It hasn't passed you by, Grif. Not at all. Your feelings may have to take a step back until Marcy deals with the sister preoccupation. I can't even imagine how you feel. You're bursting with love and having to pocket it so you can get her full attention. That even makes me sad."

"Thanks. I guess that's what I was planning, but then I asked myself if not asking her was stupid or cowardly. If she knew she was loved, then maybe the sister idea wouldn't be so important to her."

Cade released a lengthy breath. "I don't want to disillusion you, Grif, but you're talking about two totally different situations, and I'm not sure one compares to the other. You want to offer Marcy a new life, a husband and hopefully children, the legacy I've heard you talk about. But think about it, Marcy is looking for a past, a connection with someone whose blood comes from the same parents and runs through both of their veins. Family. Roots. Heritage."

Grif closed his eyes as Cade's thoughts roared through his head. "Roots. Heritage. I guess you're right. Legacy is different and family love is not the same as marital love."

"Not at all." Cade gave his shoulders a squeeze. "You choose your mate, one who fits your life, who stirs your hopes and dreams, who hangs in your mind like a familiar sweet scent that causes you to think of that person each moment you're away. That's marital love."

"I do think of her all the time. Sometimes I chuckle and sometimes I could weep for what she went through in her life. But both of these make Marcy who she is, a wonderful woman who has opened doors and brightened the world for me."

"Then you have your answer, I think."

"I do." He stuck out his hand and grasped Cade's. "Thanks for listening, Pal. I know now what I have to do."

Chapter 9

Marcy stared at the computer screen, her fingers touching the keys while she ached with tension. She'd given up on waiting, just as Grif had suggested, and had sent a message again to Lacy, her sister. She hoped. The possibility raced through her and plowed into her chest, leaving her breathless.

Grif may have been right. Not everyone runs to the computer ten times a day to look for new messages or social media comments. She'd never been that caught up in it, so why would she assume the woman with her similar DNA had any more interest in email than she had?

With Grif on her mind, she lowered her hands and lifted her cell phone. He hadn't called her in two days, and he'd acted as if he had something to talk about or maybe something important he wanted to share, but she'd paid little attention to his comments. All that occupied her mind burned an image in her head of a sister, family, someone who belonged in her world.

But even if they shared the same blood... Her shoulders rose and fell, facing the truth that even blood doesn't result in familial love or values. Studies showed that although some attributes might be influenced by genes, personalities and emotions were developed in a variety of ways.

Her phone's ringtone caused her to jump. She grasped her cell, hoping, and hit the button. "Marcy?"

"Oh, Grif, good to hear from you."

For a moment, she heard only silence. "I hope I'm not interrupting you, Marcy. I wondered how you are."

How you are? Guilt sheared through her. "I'm okay, Grif. I was thinking of you and—"

"You were? Why? Is something wrong?"

Again, her heart ached. "Nothing's wrong between you and me, Grif. I wrote to Lacy again, and I've been staying away from the phone. This time I gave her my phone number, and I didn't want to miss her call."

"Oh. Then I'll hang up. I don't want you to miss the call."

She opened her mouth to respond, but instead, she heard a click and dead silence. Her head lowered, ashamed and frustrated with herself. Grif meant so much to her. He'd been a wonderful friend—more than a friend, and she'd treated him badly without thinking.

She gazed at the phone contacts and hit his number. Her heart thudded while waiting. When she heard his voice, tears filled her eyes. "Grif, you're not a problem. I'm the problem. I've been living my life waiting. Waiting for the unknown. And why? You are more important to me than finding family. I've lived without family since my parents have been gone. You've—"

"Please don't apologize, Marcy. Yes, I miss you, but I can't imagine what it might be like to find someone who is family."

"But family with no real history. Grif, you and I have history. Let's do something tonight. Should I come over there or—"

"Are you sure?"

"Positive. I can check to see if I have something in the house to make a nice dinner."

"Don't worry about that. I'll come over around five, and we can go out somewhere. How about Stromboli's or any place you suggest."

"Stromboli's sounds great. I can't wait to see you Grif."

"Same here, Marcy."

When he ended the call, an eerie loneliness swept over her. She'd been too preoccupied with Lacy and Grif had taken a back seat. It made no sense. He'd been her life during the past months. How could she allow a stranger, someone who hadn't even responded to her contact, to push Grif from her mind.

She set the phone on her computer desk and headed to her bedroom. Since she hadn't seen Grif in a few days, she wanted to dress nicely for him. As she stared into her closet, nothing jumped out at her. Although she'd added a few western outfits to her wardrobe, her regular clothes looked drab and old as she studied them.

Brown skirt, navy dress, black slacks, white blouse, beige knit top, no patterns, nothing. She dug into her dresser drawer and found a coral top with a black trim around the collar. At least it was a color. She pulled out the top, slipped her black pants from the hanger, and shrugged. Soon, she needed to shop for clothes.

As she laid the clothing on her bed, her cell phone rang. She dug it from her pocket and eyed the unknown number. Another one of those spam calls or a marketer trying to sell her something she didn't want. She lifted her finger to end the call and then faltered. Could it be?

Her chest tightened as anticipation took a nose dive.

"Hello."

"Is this Marcy?"

The woman's voice revived her hope. "Yes, it is."

"This is Lacy."

Her heart clogged her throat. Lacy. A heavy thump pounded in her chest and her ears rang. Fearing she would faint, she settled on the edge of the bed. "Lacy, I've hoped that you would call."

"I wanted to Marcy, but… It's hard to explain. I feared if I did all my dreams would—"

"Blow up in your face? I've had the same thoughts. But I've been as anxious as you have been, I'm sure, to learn if I have family. Once I saw the DNA report. I hoped it was a sister."

"Sister? Do you think so?"

"It's a long story, but I know after I was born, my mother—our mother, I'm quite sure of that, gave her second daughter for adoption. Does that sound right to you?"

"I was adopted. I have no idea why."

Marcy ached, and she wished she'd kept her mouth shut for now about the reason for the adoption. "I've only learned a little over the past years, Lacy. I had strange memories from childhood, and I've tried putting them together to understand. I'm still not sure that I have everything right, but—"

"My mother left a note with me explaining that I would have a better life being raised by a loving family. And I did, Marcy. My parents are wonderful, and I've had a good life."

Relief washed over her, hearing her sister's revelation. "I didn't know about the note, Lacy, but I'm grateful. She was a good mother, but our problem was our father. He wanted boys not girls, and Mom only gave him girls. Me and You. When you were born, he refused to raise another girl. He was a father who wanted me to be in the background. I grew up without a sense of value or purpose, never offering my opinions or able to stand up for myself."

"That's sad." Lacy's stressed voice reflected her sadness. "I can't imagine feeling like that. Your mother…our mother gave me a wonderful gift when she let me grow up in a loving home. I'm sorry that she had to live with that kind of pressure. Your dad…our dad…made both your and our mom's lives miserable, it seems."

Marcy's stomach tightened. "But I'm happy for you, Lacy. I'm glad you had a wonderful life, and now finding you will make mine wonderful. Since Mom died and our father never offered a sense of family before he died, I've been very alone. I have a few friends, but that's not really family."

"Aren't you married, Marcy?"

Married? Marcy drew back surprised by the question and more so how she said it. "No, I never let myself have feelings for a man, fearing that I might not recognize one like our father, and end up with a life even more alone than I had."

Silence throbbed against Marcy's ear except for Lacy's soft gasp. Holding the soundless phone against her ear, her own questions arose. "Are you're married?"

"I'm engaged to a wonderful man. He teaches at the University of California campus in San Bernardino.

Another question Marcy hadn't even thought to ask. "California? Then you're not too far from me. I live in

Cottonwood, Arizona which is very close to Sedona. Maybe you've heard of its red rocks."

"I've heard that the area is very beautiful."

"It is. I wish you could see the rock formations. They are amazing, always reminding me of God's almighty creation."

"Mountains, rocks, oceans, sunrises and sunsets. Everything is God's creation. And, Marcy, I will see the rocks. Soon."

"Soon." Marcy rose from the bed, nearly choking on the word. Was Lacy telling her—?

"Roger said if you were my sister and lived close enough, he would drive me to visit, and if you were too far, he wanted me to fly." Her pitch raised. "And you're close. Maybe only six or seven hours away. We can drive."

Marcy stared into space unable to speak. She swallowed and struggled to breathe again. A sister, and she would meet her. "Lacy, when can you come? We've already waited a lifetime."

"We have." Lacy's voice lilted. "I'll let you know as soon as I talk with Roger. He'll check his work schedule. This is so exciting."

"It is. I can barely breathe."

"Don't die on me now, Sister."

Marcy found her voice and chuckled. "Wouldn't that be horrible. I promise I'll take care of myself, and you do the same. Let me know as soon as you can. I have a guest room so you can stay with me, if you want." She'd forgotten about Roger. "Or I can make a reservation somewhere if you prefer."

"I'll let you know after I talk with Roger. Marcy, thank you for making the effort to contact me. I did the

DNA to see if I could identify my nationality and any other information I could learn. Even though I wanted to connect, I never thought I'd find family. I'm beyond happy."

"So am I, Lacy. I'll be waiting for your call."

"It shouldn't be too long. Until then, I'll see you soon, Sister."

Sister. The word fluttered through her chest and down to her knees. "See you soon." Unsteady, she grasped the bed post and sank back to the mattress as her sister's voice reverberated in her head. She couldn't wait.

The excitement had unsettled her. Her chest ached while her head spun, and her energy sagged. She leaned back on the bed and fluffed the pillow. Soon. Soon she would meet her sister. That's all she could handle. She closed her eyes overcome by news she'd received.

♥

Grif changed clothes and glanced at his watch. He had a few minutes, but he'd just as soon get to Marcy's early. They could talk a little before heading out to dinner. When he stepped outside, his gaze drifted to the horizon where a sweep of pink and gold color had begun to announce the sunset. His heart swelled, wondering if tonight he might have the courage to tell Marcy how much he cared and longed for her to be his wife.

The colors deepened as he pulled into her driveway. He leaned back, waiting for her to appear as she always did when he arrived. She had a knack for being ready and near the door whenever he arrived. That added to his confidence. He believed she looked forward to seeing him.

Today she surprised him. Marcy hadn't appeared, and he tried to decide if she'd been confused about their plans. Perhaps she had gone to his house. He slipped from his SUV and hurried to the porch. He could see inside the small peep window, but he couldn't see her. Instead of ringing the bell, he tapped on the door, and after waiting with no response, he knocked. Nothing.

He reached down, his finger above the bell, but stopped. If Marcy was home, she would hear the knock. Another moment passed until his decision was made. He'd return home, and if she wasn't there. That was it. He would know that her part in his life had only been a pitiful hope heightened by his imagination.

As he drove home, anxiety knotted his neck and twisted down his spine. Though his doubt grew, he longed to see her car in his driveway. But reality smacked him when his driveway was empty. He drove to the back and parked, and when he stepped outside, the blue sky had vanished and a palette of gold, red, and violet splashed across the horizon. The end of a day, though beautiful, could be a reflection of the end of a relationship that he'd valued.

He walked into the house, headed to the kitchen and faced facts. Food meant nothing to him tonight. Though early, the only thing he could face was an attempt to sleep. He removed the clothes he'd worn for their special dinner and sat on the edge of his bed while he prayed that he could sleep. Exhaustion weighted his body. Exhaustion and utter despair.

♥

After managing to swallow some coffee and a piece of toast, Grif ambled outside and after he led the horses to the paddock, he leaned on the railing as he stared at the mountainous landscape surrounding him. He'd spent his life alone, but since Marcy had vacated his life, the loneliness grew to a deep and utter emptiness.

He'd laid his problems on Cade, and that was it. No more opening up his chest and exposing the hopeless darkness that surrounded him. Marcy had filled his life with purpose. He'd exposed his vulnerability and let her into his heart. Yet, she seemed to have walked away without looking back. She'd apparently found her family. How could he ask her to forget about the sister she longed to find and return to him?

Shame settled over him. Since he'd apparently lost Marcy, he needed someone in his life. Instead of waiting, he wanted to act now on his desire while he understood that living alone wasn't his life goal. He wanted someone who might fill his longing to have a wife and family and now his hope needed to be a priority.

He pulled his gaze away from the broad desert plain rolling to the Mingus Mountains and gazed toward Jerome in the Black Hills. If only Marcy had given him time to let her know how much he cared. And yet he prayed, somewhere out there, someone waited for him.

The rising sun's glare caused him to squint, and he turned away from the landscape. No matter what, he had his ranch, his horses and some friends who cared. Life had ups and downs, and he'd learned to deal with whatever direction it was going. At the moment, he longed for things to look up, and they would if he pulled his head out of the gloom.

Marcy hadn't called to explain, and he'd thought she would. His phone hadn't rung last night and not even a text that morning which seemed strange, but sometimes things happened. He strode away from the corral as he dug into his pocket for his cell phone. He patted both sides and reached in his single shirt pocket. Nothing. Had it fallen in the grass or—? He stopped and closed his eyes. Had he left it in the house?

With the question hanging in his mind, he hurried to the door and stepped inside. Without searching for his phone, he spotted it on a lamp table. He saw a light blinking in the corner and knew he'd missed a call or a text. When he checked the text, he had nothing, but he found success when he hit the phone button. Marcy had left a message.

His spirit lifted as he hit the voicemail button. "Grif, call me when you have a chance. I have so much to tell you."

The message lifted his spirit and without hesitation, he made the call, his pulse pumping to hear the news she had to tell him. He could only hope it was what he wanted to hear.

"Hi Marcy, I just found your message. Sorry I left my—"

"Grif, I have a sister. Lacy and I are true blood sisters, and we're going to meet. I can't believe I finally have family."

Family, something he never had. "I'm happy for you Marcy. I should have realized that something important caused you to forget our—"

"Can you imagine how thrilled I am, Grif. I've spent my life feeling sort of empty, and then a person stepped into my life, and not just a person."

His hurt faded as he pictured her eyes glinting with joy, while his expectation rose. "Not any person?"

"No, a sister. My very own sister."

His foolish hope and dreams caved in and crushed his heart. The joy in her voice, like a knife wound, caused him pain. Yet he wanted to feel her happiness about her sister, but he couldn't. Since their past relationship had brought him happiness, he wished he could jump in with words rejoicing in pleasure for her.

Instead, his trust and expectation failed. He'd been ignorant to think that Marcy really cared about him. No one had ever come into his life until he'd met her, and she'd given him the desire to marry and have children. He'd lived alone with his horses and a few friends and that had been enough. Why had he allowed himself to take a chance on more?

"I suppose you're tired of hearing me blabber, Grif. I'm so flustered that I need to take a break and get myself calmed down."

He found the words he hadn't been able to face. "I'm happy for you, Marcy. I hope you and your sister have a wonderful relationship. I can only imagine how amazing this has been. I wish you blessings and good things from now on." Without a goodbye, he ended the call. He placed his phone back on the table with no desire to talk with anyone, not even Marcy.

Outside the blue sky streaming with sunlight didn't brighten his mood. Something had to change, but what? If he didn't have the ranch responsibility, he longed to get away, to travel to places he'd never been and enjoy a world he'd never known.

Again, he scanned the distant, the powerful mountain range that surrounded him. Could anything be more beautiful? He'd always loved living in the Southwest. Here, he could take a short ride and gaze at the red rocks of Sedona, always spectacular no matter how often he stared at the unique formations.

Instead of grieving, he bolstered his spirit and headed for the paddock. The horses were fine, and rather than wasting time, Western Outlet dropped into his thoughts. He hadn't been there for a couple of weeks and it was time. Time to do a lot of things he hadn't done while hoping and waiting and hoping some more. The decision to give up the romantic dreams that had wrapped around his heart now settled in his mind. He could do it when it came to rejection. That was the reason, he'd avoided relationships. Friendships were all he could handle.

Assured that the horses had water and hay available in the paddock, he climbed into his SUV and headed into town. He pulled behind the shop, parked and entered through the back door. When he stepped inside the shop, his clerk Alex spun around.

"Whoa, you scared me."

Grif chuckled. "Unless you're planning to the rob the place, there's no need to be scared."

Alex shook his head with a grin. "I thought I'd wait until you had millions. What's a few thousand dollars."

Grif patted his back. "Good thinking, Alex. I'll keep that in mind."

Alex shook his head again. "Do you want something or just dropping by?"

"Nothing particular. Do we need to order anything? How are sales?"

"Actually, sales have been good." Alex shrugged. "Not sure why, but the Western clothing has been a big seller. And I did sell some tack to a couple of new ranchers. They were happy to find the store."

"Great. Don't forget if they want something we

don't have, we can order it. I get a better price than they will ordering by themselves."

Alex nodded. "Right."

Grif stepped away and noticed a buyer he'd missed when he entered. The woman looked familiar, but no name came to him. His interest moved him closer, though his staring made him uncomfortable. But his curiosity won out. When she looked up, he recognized her. "Iris, how are you?" He extended his hand and closed the distance between them. "When did you get back in town?"

"My dad has been sick, Grif, and he asked me if I could spare some time." Before she lowered her head, he spotted a mist in her eyes. "I felt rotten. Just disgusted with my lack of concern."

"Don't say that, Iris. If he didn't let you know that he was sick, then you shouldn't be ashamed. You're here now, and that's what counts."

She gazed at him with teary eyes and yet a look of comfort on her face. "Thanks. I love my dad, and I haven't visited him enough to show him that I care."

He rested his hand on her shoulder. "If I know that you care about your him, I'm sure your dad knows too. You don't live here anymore so it's impossible to be on top of things. He loves you, and I'm sure he's just happy that you are here."

"My brother arrived the day after I did, so it's giving me some time to do a few things and he's planning to stay a while, so I'll return home and come back later. Meanwhile, I'm so glad I ran into you."

"So am I. We've been friends a long time." His memory flashed back to days when they went riding and laughing. Iris was open and interesting with her stories to tell, but she also listened and showed pleasure being with the people she knew. She was also an attractive woman. "What else are you doing today?"

"Just picking up a few things, and I think I'll go somewhere for lunch."

"Lunch? Are you alone or are you—"

"Just me. Why? Are you hungry, too?"

He grinned. "As a matter of fact, I am."

"Then I don't think I'll be eating alone. What do you say?"

"I say great. I have free time today and nothing is better than having time to talk with you." Though he'd said the words, the image in his head became Marcy. Why couldn't she be as open and carefree as Iris?

"Let me pay for these things, and then we can find a place to eat."

"And talk. We have a few years to cover."

"This could lead to dinner." She chuckled and placed her palm over his hand that rested on her shoulder.

He hadn't felt as relaxed with a woman since Marcy and then her preoccupation with her sister stole her away. He'd been lonely. But running into Iris seemed to open the door and fill that empty feeling he'd lived with recently.

Chapter 10

While Iris paid the bill, Grif wandered around the store and eyed the merchandize as he estimated what needed to be reordered. He jotted down the items and asked Alex to take care of the order. Facing his struggle, Grif wanted to take care of himself—his sadness and discouragement. Really his hurt. Iris had been a long-time friend and his confidence rose that she would stave off the pity-party going on in his head.

"Ready?" He watched her slip her wallet into her handbag.

She grinned and nodded. "I just heard my stomach answer that question. I'm more than ready." She grasped her packages and stepped toward him. "I'll drive so I can put these in the car."

"No need. Put them in your car, and we can walk to a restaurant. I think there are three within a half a block."

She grinned as he opened the door and held it for her as she stepped outside. In a moment, her packages were locked in the trunk and he slipped his arm around her shoulders and gave her a quick hug before pointing to the café only a few steps away.

Grif opened the café door, and they were guided to

a booth along the windows. They perused the menu and placed their order as another young woman stopped at their table with two tall glasses of water.

When she left, Grif turned his attention to Iris. "It's great to see you, Iris."

"It's nice to see you, too, Grif. It's been a long time."

"Months. You're right. But nothing has changed since you were here. I'm still doing my duties at the ranch, and—"

"And still single, it appears." She arched an eyebrow.

He questioned her look. "Yes, but I didn't realize that singleness could show on someone's face."

"But it does, Grif. I can look into your eyes and the look hasn't changed. I see eyes that might glint with happiness, but yours seem to send out the same look of 'I'm trying to look happy but I'm not.'"

He closed his eyes a moment not to hide his feelings, but to gather his thoughts. His brain sent a message that was too true. He couldn't hide much from Iris. They'd known each other too long. He shrugged. "I would be happy, Iris, but something happened that I don't understand."

Her eyes widened. "Really? I've never known you to be that concerned about anything but your horses and the ranch. Are you having problems? Ailing horses? Financial? What's troubling you?

He drew in a breath, concerned about how much he wanted to tell her. And yet he'd always been open with Iris. "The ranch and finances…even the store is doing well. It's not that. It's…it's me and my future."

"Future?" Her frown deepened. "I've never heard

you be concerned about the future, Grif. Maybe it's not the horses. Are you ill?"

A grin slipped to his lips even though he saw her concern. "I'm as healthy as the horses, Iris. It's thoughts about a legacy. I've begun to face my situation and realize—"

"You're single. You have no heirs to give your property to. No wife. No children. It's about time the situation struck you. I wondered if it would dawn on you one day, and I always prayed it came before it was too late. You know that you're my dearest friend."

"You are mine, too, Iris." The awareness softened his heart.

An expression settled on her face that he didn't recognize. Then it grew to a grin. "I'm going to be honest, Grif, and please don't take this wrong. But I often wondered if our relationship would become more than a friendship." The grin grew to a smile that lit her face. "But then I gave it more thought, I knew I treasured your friendship more than anything. You're more like a brother than a lover, Grif."

He nodded as relief swept through him. "I sometimes asked myself if that might happen, but just as you said, you're a sister more than a life partner, Iris, and I'm so happy you feel the same way as I do. It would devastate me if I hurt you in any way. You've been a strength in our friendship, and I would never want to lose that."

"Me neither, Grif. But I've hoped that one day you would find someone to—"

The waitress appeared at their side, and by the time, she'd delivered their meals, the conversation faded away. In some ways, Grif was glad it did.

They delved into their lunch, but it didn't take long for Iris to lower her fork to the plate, and gaze at him again. "Before we were interrupted, I don't want to lose my thought. Grif, I've hoped that eventually you'd find someone important, someone to—"

Grif raised his palm. "I did. It surprised me, but I did find someone that made me think of marriage and a family."

A deep frown spread to Iris's face. "Where is she?"

"She's still here, but something happened to change our relationship and I don't think it will ever come back as strong as it was. That's what I meant about thinking I would be happy if…"

Confusion replaced her frown. "I don't understand. What happened? How could that be?"

Grif lowered his head as her question tore through his mind as it had done a hundred times. "It's a long story, and maybe it's my fault."

"I'm still confused." Her eyes searched his.

His lungs drained but he grasped his wits and admitted he had only one way to resolve her curiosity, and Iris deserved to know. "I can try to make it short, but it's a long story, Iris. Let's finish our meal before it's cold, okay?"

Iris slipped her hand over his and gave it a squeeze. "We can sit here until dinner time if necessary."

They focused on their plates until they'd both set down their forks and the waitress returned to refill their coffee. Iris leaned back after sipping the hot brew and gazed at him as if she were studying a piece of artwork that she didn't understand.

Though not sure if he could tell the story correctly, he tried to relax and began the long tale, how he'd met

Marcy, how their relationship had grown slow but sure, and how he'd let her down when her sister appeared.

As she listened, Iris's expression altered from grins to frowns to frustration, and when he finished, he left her with a look he couldn't identify.

"Grif, I still don't understand. She found a sister through DNA that she'd never known, and now she's walked away from you? That doesn't make sense, does it? A family isn't a partner for life who will love you and keep you in his care. Why would she walk away?"

He eyed her without a solid answer. Had she walked away or had her excitement made her forget their dinner plans? How could he be upset while she was thrilled to find her sister? "Iris, I don't know, and as I think about it, I'm may be the one who backed away."

"But why? This is the woman who'd opened your eyes to love and marriage, to having a family which is even more than a legacy. It's a gift to have children and a wife who loves you."

His head hung lower than it had. She was right. He'd acted like a child, angry at Santa for not bringing a toy that he wanted. But how could he explain that to Iris?"

"You said she stood you up at a dinner you'd planned. Is that what upset you so much? I can understand that you were concerned and surprised that she'd forgotten, but when she told you about her sister and her excitement of having a real family, how could you still be angry?"

His air rattled in his lungs. "I don't know, Iris. I'm ashamed that I didn't rejoice with her. I tried when I realized how foolish I was being, but I'm not sure that was enough."

"If she cares about you as you thought she did, Grif, Marcy will return just as she had been. Right now, she's overwhelmed by finding a sister. That's family, and everyone wants family. If you think about it, that's what you want, isn't it? A family, a wife and hopefully children."

He forced his head upward, managing to hide his frustration. He hoped he'd hid it. "That's true. I'm not used to romance, Iris, and I didn't know how to handle being forgotten. That's how I saw it. The horses never let me forget to feed them, but then Marcy isn't a horse."

"Now you're talking. I'm glad you know the difference. And another difference is to put on Marcy's shoes."

"What?" He looked down at his size eleven boots, trying to imagine.

Iris chuckled. "I'm talking about putting yourself in her position. Imagine learning that you have a brother you never knew. What emotion would you feel? How excited would you be that you might forget to make a phone call or drop by a friend's house as you'd promised."

He nodded, unable to do anything else. Iris had flooded him with reality. He didn't have anyone special in his life except Marcy, and her distraction struck him in a way he'd never expected. "You're right. I see where I've gone wrong. Very wrong. I need to do something about it, and I pray it's not too late."

"Trust me. You're not too late, Grif. Get your head together. Think it through and then take action. Let her know that she's important to you. That you feel lonely without her. She's known loneliness. We all have, and she'll understand."

"I hope you're right."

"I am, Grif. I'm a woman, and I know what women do."

He couldn't argue that point, so he tucked away his thoughts and listened. He gave her a nod and took another swig of coffee, hoping to change the subject, and as he weighed his questions, he decided to ask one that had bothered him.

"Iris, you do understand women, but I know that, just like men are different, all women aren't the same. So, let me ask your opinion on something."

"Okay. I'll answer if I think I can help."

"I'm crazy about Marcy, but one thing that concerns me is her inability to try something new. It's as if she's afraid. I do know that her father raised her with the philosophy that a woman is seen and not heard. She and her mother never questioned anything from what she's told me. They did as he said and kept quiet."

Iris's neck swiveled back and forth as if she couldn't believe what she had heard. "I can't even imagine being raised with that idea drilled in my head, Grif. We are influenced by our past, and maybe Marcy thinks her father was protecting her from being hurt in some way so she's afraid to try new things. Or maybe she can't imagine new experiences. You believe she has feelings for you, and I'm sure you're right, but even that would be a new experience and one that she has to learn to accept."

"I didn't think of that. She was slow to show her feelings, and she's still very tentative about her emotions."

" Then what things does she avoid? That is if you

don't mind telling me."

"Not at all. You can guess that one thing was riding a horse, but she finally got on it and she'll go out if we trot. Nothing faster." He looked away to get his thoughts in order. "I taught her friend, Ally how to improve her riding. She'd learned most everything from Cade, you know him, I think."

"Sure. He owns a ranch in Sedona, right?"

"Yes, and he married Allysa. Everyone calls her Ally, and she is good friends with Marcy. They both work at the Verde Valley Medical Center."

"What does Marcy say when you've asked her to try something new?"

"When it was horseback riding, she said she'd do things with both feet on the ground."

"That makes sense. She grew up with little leeway for experiencing things. She's afraid of new things. I think it's just time, Grif. If she's trotting on the horse now, it won't be long and she'll be able to ride with more confidence. Time is what you need to remember."

He wanted to roll his eyes, but she made sense. He'd be patient although that wasn't something he did well. "Thanks. I'll try to do that."

"And Grif, if that's your only complaint, I think you've found someone worth fighting for."

His pulse skipped as he pictured life with a wife and, perhaps, children. The vision, though a fantasy, caused him to weigh the real possibility of being a husband and father. A year ago, that image would never have entered his mind. Today, everything had changed.

♥

Marcy gazed at her sister for the hundredth time, still disbelieving. Her chest ached with the desire to cry in pure happiness. For so many years, she'd lived with an emptiness that knotted her view of life, and she had yet to fully deal with the old Marcy, women are seen but not heard. Her father had dealt a blow that had warped her viewpoint.

Lacy studied her a minute as a frown merged on her face. "Marcy, are you still hurting from our father's horrible attitude?"

"I wish I could say no, but I can't. I'm sitting here so thrilled that you're visiting me, Lacy, and yet I tend to wait for the hammer to strike and destroy what could be wonderful memories."

Lacy rose and hurried to her side. She sat on the arm of the chair. "Please, Marcy. Think of ways you can block those horrors. If I had experienced our father's horrendous attitude toward women, my life would be ruined too, but I was blessed in a strange way. Having our mother give me up for adoption was truly a gift."

Marcy's pulse skipped. "I've never looked at it like that. I thought you'd be wounded never knowing your birth mother."

A frown settled on Lacy's face. "Strange, but it never struck me to feel that way. I was raised by a man and woman who loved me dearly and opened the world to me in amazing ways. Not by giving me everything I wanted, but by helping me see that I could be my own worst enemy unless I learned to love myself so that I could be a happy and whole person. My adoption was a gift. These people wanted me. They chose me. They gave me unending love."

Marcy sat a moment amazed at Lacy's explanation. Lacy's life had been so much better than her own. How could she even think that being adopted caused her a problem? "You make so much sense, Lacy. I wish I had the opportunity you did to realize that I have the right to attitudes and feelings. That I can speak out and be the person I want to be."

"If you believe that, then it's not too late. You have a man who has encouraged you to grow and experience life. He's never told you to be seen and not heard. Right?"

Marcy nodded. "Never. He's been encouraging all the way."

"Then take advantage of the blessing. Open up to him. Try to spread your wings. They may have been clipped years ago, but not today. Your wings have grown, and you have a man who is there to catch you if you stumble. Take hold of the reins, Marcy. Give him a chance to help you make the changes that you need, so you can be that whole person you want to be."

Tears blurred in her eyes as she reached toward Lacy. "Thank you, sister." Amid her tears she managed to smile. Hearing the word sister touched her heart with joy and gratitude.

Lacy leaned closer and gave her a hug. "Now, I know you're happy to see me, but I have to leave soon. Tomorrow actually."

"That soon?" A sweep of reality washed over her. "I understand, Sis. We both have lives, jobs, and responsibilities, but I don't want to be away from you without an occasional visit."

"We can visit, and don't forget, there are phone calls. Do you have an app on your phone to see each other face to face as we talk? That would be great?"

"If I don't, I'll get it." Marcy chuckled. "I'm not

only slow about experiencing new things, I'm very backward when it comes to technology. But if there's such a thing, I'll get it."

Lacy added her snicker to the conversation. "Good. And next time, you can come and visit me."

"I'd love to." Marcy opened her arms and embraced her sister with a comfort that she'd never known until she met Grif. He made loving easy. She grasped. For the first time, she knew she did love Grif more than she could say, and before she lost him, she'd better make big changes in her life.

"Lacy, I can't tell you how much this meeting has meant to me, and how much our conversations have made me aware of so many things that I didn't see. Thank you."

"Thank you, Sis. The feeling is mutual." She drew Marcy into a bear hug. "I'm also dating a man that I think is the one who is meant for me, but through our talks I see that I need to be more open too. I haven't said much about my feelings, not wanting to be hurt, but that will change. When I get back, I will open my heart in the same way he has."

"You mean he's told you how he feels, but you haven't let him know that—"

"You and I came from the same parents, Marcy. I think genes also influence our behavior as well as how we are raised." She shrugged. "I've hesitated, but not anymore." Lacy arched a brow. "And I hope that you won't hesitate either."

Marcy lifted her hand against her heart. "I promise. I need to let him know. It will still take a little time, but I'm going to first surprise him with becoming more adventurous. He'll see the difference, and I know he'll love it."

"And will love you for it. Wishing you blessings, Marcy."

"Same here. I'm anxious to meet the one who'll become your husband too."

A huge smile grew on Lacy's face. "He'll be surprised when I get back. I'm a changed woman, and I'm so glad that we both finally saw the light."

Chapter 11

Grif sat across from Iris in a booth at Stromboli's, happy they'd seen each other again. Friendships were precious, and he and Iris had always been food friends. They had never considered a romantic relationship. She was too much like a sister, and she'd said that he'd been like a brother. And now he had good reason that it could never happen. He'd fallen in love with Marcy, the kind of forever love he'd begun to dream about.

"You mentioned leaving soon, Iris. I pray your dad can get through this bad time. I know the pressure it must put on you."

Iris stared at the table and drew in a breath before lifting her eyes to his. "Thanks, Grif. I pray the same. I know I'll lose him one day. It's something we all face, but I'm not ready." She grinned. "None of us are."

"You're right, but as we age, the life we have becomes a gift, one we treasure, especially when we think of the time we've wasted." He reached over and touched her hand. "Don't follow my bad example Iris. I realize that being single can eventually become lonely for some of us. I own a horse ranch, a store and so many things that I want to leave to someone, and without a wife or children, I have a legacy with nowhere to go."

"The thought has passed through my mind, too, Grif, but I try to push it away. I can't make miracles happen, and I will wait and see if the Lord has a plan for me. I would like to be a mom one day, I think." She chuckled. "Although I hear some of my friends with children roll their eyes when I've said that. They remind me children don't always improve with age. The problems can just get bigger."

Although he grinned, he had a different take. "I'm sure, but we all have to take our chances."

"I suppose we do." Again, she drew in a deep breath. "The food was good here, Grif. Thanks for inviting me, but I'm watching the time, and I need to get moving. I'm leaving in the morning and I still have a few things to do with dad, plus pack."

"I understand. I hope, too, that your dad improves. And I'm especially grateful that we ran into each other. It's good to see long-time friends."

"It is Grif." She rose and stepped into his arms.

He gave her a bear hug. "Let me know when you're back in town, okay?"

"I will. It's been so nice seeing you. It sort of brings back old times."

"It does, Grif. Those are sweet memories."

"They are. You take care of yourself, and I'll see you the next time you come to town." He lowered his head and kissed her cheek.

She gave him a squeeze and a wave and headed toward the door. As he followed her with his eyes, his heart stood still. He spotted Marcy jerking her head away from them and beating Iris to the door. Before he could move, Marcy had vanished.

♥

Marcy sat alone staring at her tray in the hospital cafeteria. She longed to forget what she'd seen at Stromboli's, but she'd been unable to wipe the vision from her memory. Ally's voice caught her off guard, and she jumped.

"Sorry, I didn't mean to scare you. Do you mind if I join you?"

"Not at all." Marcy tapped the tabletop beside her. "In fact, you'll be a good distraction."

"Distraction." Ally shifted her gaze right and left with a frown. "Who are you avoiding or thinking about?"

"Can't you guess?"

"Ahh, Grif." Ally's frown ease. "But I still don't understand."

"Neither do I." Moisture filled her eyes, and she pressed her lips together to avoid letting a sob escape. "I saw Grif with a woman, but not any woman, one he hugged and kissed on the cheek."

"Grif? I have no idea who that might be. He's never dated that I know of, and I really thought that you and—"

"So did I, Ally. I never thought I'd fall for anyone, not with my upbringing, but I did. Now how do I undo those feelings?"

Ally pressed her palm on Marcy's hand. "Don't do anything rash. You'll be sorry, Marcy." She shook her head. "You need to hear Grif's story first. I'm sure he has a good explanation, but if you react first, you could do damage. You don't want to do that. I know you don't."

"But how can he excuse what I saw, Ally. He could come up with some wild story. He could lie, and I'm stupid enough to believe him."

"You are far from stupid, Marcy. Don't say that. You're an intelligent woman. Sometimes things look one way, but they can be totally different from your imagined explanation. Wait and hear his story."

Losing the battle, tears rolled down Marcy's cheeks. "I can't imagine—"

"No imagining. You need the facts. Forget your imagination. It's fiction. Please."

"I don't know. I really don't." Marcy closed her eyes, her lips pursed as she tried to weigh her options. Either she accused him or, as Ally said, she could wait to hear his response. "I'll wait, Ally, but I'm not sure if my heart is in it."

"Waiting offers you a chance to hear what he has to say. The other option is to walk away. But if you love Grif with your heart, then you'll give him a chance. That's what love means, Marcy. To listen, to talk, and to forgive. Love is worth it. I know from experience."

Ally's words washed over Marcy. Ally did understand. She and Cade had been married for a few months, and their love seemed brighter than the day they married.

She lowered her head, ashamed of her attitude and her doubts. "Grif has always been honest. At least, he seemed honest to me…so you're right. I need to listen and not come to a conclusion before hearing his side."

Tension lifted from Ally's face, and her tension lifted too when she saw her friend's relieved expression.

"I'm happy for both of us, Marcy. You've been a

friend for a long time, and I've never known you to make assumptions with that much determination. Deciding to wait and listen makes me happy, and I'm also happy for you. I fear you could have damaged or even lost something precious."

Marcy studied Ally's face. "You mean Grif?"

"Who else? As I said, love is patient and waits for an explanation. And as important, love forgives. Remember that the Lord forgives us for our multitude of sins. You'll know if you need forgiveness once you learn the truth of what happened."

"You're right, Ally. It's in the Bible." Sadness weighted in her chest. "I jumped to conclusions and doing that reminds me of my father's words. 'A woman should be seen and not heard.' Maybe he was right."

"No. Never. A woman has as much right to be heard as anyone, but your mistake was to assume what had happened and then you felt hurt before you knew the truth. Truth makes us free, Marcy. Remember that." Ally stepped closer and embraced her.

"Thank you. Thank you so much. I've been unsure of myself too long, and I need to accept that I can be loved by someone. I grew up thinking that love had to be earned, and I didn't have the capacity to earn it."

"Oh, Marcy." Ally stared at her, shaking her head. "Never, ever think that again. You are so worthy of love. Grif is a great guy, and I'm sure he loves you. Love happens because we see qualities that we admire in someone. We see attributes we want to have, and we respect them in the other person. They stir our heart with their laughter and their tears. We feel lost without them."

"Lost without them." She repeated Ally's words and

listened to her explanation. "I do feel very lost now that I've enjoyed his company. Maybe he feels the same." She lowered her head recalling her actions when she'd found her sister.

"Ally, when I learned I had a sister, I walked away from Grif, and I'd been spending quality time with him. I was so happy and surprised to learn that I had a sister that I forgot about his feelings. Maybe that's what's happened now. Maybe the woman is a friend from his past or even present that I've never met. I can't believe I've allowed myself to get riled over an event that could have a simple answer."

"Good awareness, Marcy." Ally gave her a hug. "Don't try to figure it out but do what you said and be honest with him. Ask questions if he doesn't offer answers. But I think he will."

Pressure lifted from her chest as she reviewed Ally's comments. "Thanks so much for helping me see what is most likely the truth. I'm afraid my past tends to cling to me, and I pray that one day, it will fade and be gone. I want to trust others and I want to trust myself. I want to believe that I am worthy and loveable."

Ally smiled. "You are worthy and loveable. Please believe me. I wouldn't say it if it weren't the truth. I'm an honest person, Marcy."

"I know you are, and I'm grateful for your wise thoughts. I'm very glad you're my friend."

♥

The past few days had been horrible. Grif fed and exercised the horses. He'd spent time at the store working doing anything he could to tick off the hours, and then he went home and stared into space. Marcy had shot from the Stromboli's as if the fire alarm went off in the building. He knew she'd seen him, or it appeared that she had, but what had she seen? He'd kissed Iris's cheek. That was it, but then if he'd seen her with a man kissing her check, how would he feel?

Confusion reigned in his head. Marcy had almost vanished from his life, and he tried to understand her excitement about learning she had a sister. The situation made him happy for her, and yet she hadn't really shared it with him, but maybe she needed the time alone with her sister. But even so, she could have called and talked about her excitement, maybe even apologize for not seeing him. But she hadn't done either.

He tossed his back against the recliner and closed his eyes. Never having dated someone he cared about until Marcy came along placed him in an embarrassing position. He had no experience at all in the rules of dating or even more than dating. He'd thought she cared about him, maybe even loved him. He knew he loved her, or thought he did. Lacking experience made him guess what his feelings really meant.

Air emptied his lungs and his good sense. Though he wasn't a genius, he believed that he was a capable man with a good business sense and with the ability to love. He'd always had good feelings about his friends, a kind of love that wasn't romantic but showed him what relationships meant and how they grew and became more and more precious. If friendship grew in meaning, then love had to be stronger and even more treasured.

But had he been deluded? His feelings for Marcy might not have been reciprocated, even though he thought they were.

A lump formed in his chest, and he pressed his hand against the ache. No, he couldn't have been wrong.

Marcy had kissed him back. She'd spent time with him and even tried to be brave about learning new things. Riding on horseback when he knew she was frightened had given him confidence that she cared.

He pulled his body forward and gasped for air. Whatever happened, he wanted to understand it, so if Marcy didn't make contact, he would. He had to.

He rose from the recliner and headed for the last place he'd seen his cell phone. When he found it on the kitchen table, he noticed a light blinking in the corner. That meant someone had tried to contact him. His chest tightened again. Could it be?

When he opened his cell phone, he checked the calls and his pulse bounded through his chest. Marcy had called, and he'd missed it. He checked the time of the call. It had been an hour earlier. Not wanting to wait a second, he tapped the phone and held his breath as it rang.

"Grif?"

She'd recognized his number. "Hi, Marcy. My phone was on the table and I was in the other room. Sorry I missed your call."

"I'm glad you called back. I want to…I need to apologize, Grif."

He froze. "Apologize?"

"It's hard for me to sort through everything that's happened, but I know—"

"Your sister was here for a while. Is that what you mean?" He prayed it wasn't someone else.

"It's even more than that, Grif, and I'm ashamed."

He sank into a kitchen chair. She'd met someone else. He knew it. "Marcy, please don't…" Air drained from his chest. Don't what? Don't tell me? He dragged in fresh air and grasped for courage. "Just tell me who it is. What happened?"

"Who it is? You know who it was. My sister was here, and I wasn't myself. I've never been so thrilled about anything until learning I had a sibling. I let everything that's important to me step back, and I focused on my new finding. But that wasn't fair, Grif. You mean the world to me, and I hope you can forgive me."

Her apology, especially her comment, 'You mean the world to me', soared through his mind. "Forgive you? Because of your sister?"

"Yes, who else? I've missed you, Grif. I'm grateful my commonsense has returned. You do mean the world to me, and I didn't even have the courtesy of introducing you to my sister." Her shoulders lifted with a deep breath. "But she'll be back, and I promise I'll introduce you then. I want you to meet her. It's an amazing experience to meet someone that is part of my life and yet someone I've never known."

"I understand. I'm sure it was a difficult and yet a great experience." His words seemed inadequate after they left him.

"Yes, I was scared but now I'm thrilled. She's like me in some ways, and she said something that I'd never thought about. Even though we were raised by different parents, we still carry genetic qualities—good and bad from our birth parents. I hope you know what I mean?"

"I do. Is she skittish about learning new things?"

"She is or was. We both agreed to stretch our necks and our minds. If not, life will pass us by."

"Not if I have anything to say about it."

She chuckled and hearing it lifted his spirit.

"Lacy and I agreed that we'll both be braver and more willing to learn new things. I've started already, haven't I?"

"You have. I can't deny that. Seeing you on horseback has been a special experience for me. You always said you wanted to keep your feet on the ground."

"Right, but at least horseback means my feet aren't too far from the ground. It's not like going up in a hot air balloon."

"Ahh." Grif grasped the idea and tucked it away. "Would that be so bad?"

"Are you kidding?"

This time he laughed. "No, your feet would still be on something solid. Think of an airplane."

"I've never been on an airplane either, Grif, so that's not a good example."

"Really?" He'd never given that a thought.

"Really."

"Wow, you're missing out on some great experiences. But...I know it takes time. Anyway, I'm not so worried about where your feet are except, I'd love them standing next to me."

Silence wrapped around him. "Marcy?"

"I'm sorry, Grif. I was thinking that I not only want to be standing next to you, but I want to be in your arms. I feel safe there."

"How about tonight? Can we get together?"

"I'm working late tonight, but maybe if you don't mind coming over around seven. I could cook dinner for us."

"How about if I take you out, or bring something in? Would that work?"

"Whichever is best for you. My biggest wish is to see you."

He pictured her smile. "And seeing you is my biggest wish too. I'll be there around seven."

"Good, and thank you, Grif, for listening. I feared you'd hang up or not call me when you noticed that I called you."

"I wouldn't do that, Marcy. I'm all for waiting to hear what happened."

"I'm working on that, too. I had a long talk with Ally, but I'll tell you when I see you."

"Around seven."

"Around seven, Grif."

When he ended the call, he stood a moment staring at the phone as his curiosity rose. A long talk with Ally. What could that mean?

♥

Marcy paced her bedroom, checking and re-checking the mirror. Her nerves rattled every bone, and she hoped that she could be herself and be honest. If he didn't mention the woman, she had to, but how?

The kiss and hug had glued to her memory no matter how hard she tried to convince herself it was nothing. But hugs and kisses aren't nothing. "Stop." Hearing her voice took her aback, but it did stop her. Thinking could get out of control. She would see him very soon, and then she would get her answers. That is if she had the courage.

She eyed her watch and her heart skipped. Five more minutes and he would be there. Instead of pacing, she plopped onto the mattress edge, then rose again to pick out a sweater to match her outfit. Evenings often became cooler in late summer. She hung the cardigan over her arm, grasped her handbag, and managed to amble into the living room, trying to convince herself that everything would be fine.

When she heard the slam of a car door, her pulse tripped. She paused, her eyes glued to the door until she heard a knock. The tap had a meaning. Grif never rang the doorbell. Mustering control, she managed a slow walk to the door and pulled it open. "Grif. It's nice to see you." She shuddered at her unnatural welcome. She shifted her gaze toward her handbag. "I'm ready if you want to get going."

He stood a moment, a scowl crinkling his brow and then extended his index finger and grasped the door handle. She backed up as he stepped inside. "It's more than nice to see you, Marcy."

She shrank from his jibe, and yet she deserved it. "I'm sorry Grif. I didn't mean to say something that sounded so negative."

"It's not like you, but I understand. But before we leave, I want to get something off my chest."

Air streamed from her lungs. Seeing his serious expression, she froze. "Is something wrong, Grif?"

"Not really, but I want to explain something before you ask." Tension pulled at his jaw. "When I was leaving Stromboli's, I was surprised to see you dart out of the restaurant without speaking to me, but then, it dawned on me. You saw me with Iris. I'd hugged her and kissed her cheek, and I'm afraid you may have misconstrued the meaning. Iris is a long-time friend. She's in town to be with her father who's been ill. I haven't seen her for years, but we were good friends. Friends, Marcy. That's it."

She stared at him a moment, searching the rising

tension on his face and the hurt in his eyes. Wishing she could fall through the floor, she fought for breath.

Her voice failed her, but she had to say something. "Grif, I'm ashamed of myself. I'm more than sorry, but sorries don't make things better. I jumped to conclusion. Instead of using good sense, I created a situation that wasn't real. It was my fear that I'd lost you."

"Lost me?"

"I neglected you so badly when my sister came and—"

"Don't you think I understood that, Marcy. Yes, I didn't like it, because I missed you too, but I wasn't open with you either. I harbored the hurt, and soon it became the old 'mountain and mole hill' situation. When we hang on to frustration or anger or anything, it grows. It becomes worse than it really is. I did that. I felt sorry for myself and began to question your feelings and then my own."

"My feelings never changed, Grif. Never. You mean too much to me. You've put up with my fears, and idiosyncrasies without walking away. Instead you've tried to help me, and I hope that I have changed enough to let you know that I want to be the person I should be. Not the scaredy-cat that I'd been most of my life."

"I didn't walk away, because I care about you, Marcy. I care for you multiplied by a thousand." He glanced away a moment, closed his eyes, but then opened them and faced her. "Instead of reliving what happened, let's make up for lost time. You've eased up on your old ways, your unsureness, your unresponsiveness. Lately, you've started to live the way

God meant you to be. I'm grateful seeing you able to enjoy things and speak out. That's what we both need."

"You're right, Grif. I unwrapped the mummy from the crypt. I don't want to be bound in my own horrible thoughts or memories. I want to learn to be a whole person without restraints."

"You're on your way, Marcy." He raised his hand and pressed it on her cheek. His cool palm ran across her jaw and slid to the nap of her neck where his fingers brushed through her hair before he drew her closer. "I long to hold you in my arms every day when you're not with me, and I pray that you feel the same."

"You know I do." She drew even closer and circled his back with her arms. As she tilted her head upward, she guided her mouth to his while exploring the soft yet urgent pressure of his lips on hers. She'd longed for the freedom to act on her dream, and today, she'd ended another fear.

She eased back, dragging air into her lungs, but Grif clung to her, his lips moving against hers, his heart beating against hers in the same rhythm. When he lessened his hold, his eyes searched hers. "I could say I'm sorry, Marcy, but I'm not. I've wanted to hold you close and kiss you the way I've wanted to kiss you fully for a long time, but I didn't want to scare you." His palm again touched her cheek. "Do you trust me?"

"Yes, you know I do. You've been honest, thoughtful, patient, and kind. Why would I not trust you?" She raised her hands and cupped his cheeks. "Grif, I feel secure with you more than any man I've ever known. You've respected me and put up with me and all my backward ways. Now I want to be the kind of woman that I long to be, especially with you. I hope you're willing to help me."

His eyes looked misty, and it touched her heart. With his cheek still cupped in her hands, she tiptoed upward and kissed him again.

"Marcy, you are the dearest person I know. I don't want to push you to try one thing after another. I want you to let me know what you want to change, and I promise to help you. If you want to be the person you've become now, still a bit timid but ninety times different, then I'm happy with your choice."

Her heart skipped with his offer. She'd covered her anxiety often when she agreed to do new things, but after she had the experience, her fear turned to pride. She'd took steps and had grown.

Chapter 12

Marcy carried her tray through the hospital cafeteria looking for Ally. She finally spotted her alone and gave her a nod as she approached. "For a minute, I thought you were already here and gone." She sat across from her at the small table and eyed her lunch choice. "I could have skipped lunch today."

Ally's head snapped upward, her brow furrowed. "Why? Are you sick?"

"No, not physically. Sometimes I think my brain isn't working. I don't know, Ally. I make a mess out of too many things."

"What?" Ally shook her head, her brow furrowed. "What are you talking about?" She held up her hand. "Oh, Marcy, I'm sorry. Really sorry. I forgot you were going to talk with Grif. I'm guessing it didn't go as you hoped. What happened?" She rested her hand on Marcy's arm.

"Nothing bad happened. It's just me. I should be smiling, but the more I think about the situation, the more I realize that I'm still a mess. I can take something wonderful and turn it into something—"

"Don't say it, Marcy." Ally's pitch and volume rose. "Don't tell me your father was right. It's not true.

Women should be seen and heard not the other way around. Your father was wrong. I'd hoped that..."

Tears blurred Marcy's eyes seeing Ally's expression. Ally cared, yet she continued to be a horrible, confused mess, even though she knew her friend really cared. "I'd hoped I'd let his words fade, too. I've hashed it over so many times, and I think I get rid of my father's voice, but then I let down my guard, and it's back again."

"What caused that to happen, Marcy? Whatever it is, let it go. Block it. When it starts to fill your mind, say a prayer."

Wiping tears from her cheeks, Marcy raised her chin. "You're right. I want to let it go, and I have no real reason to allow it back into my brain." She lowered her eyes and shook her head. "Grif has been nothing but loving to me, and I should be joyful and happy. Instead I doubt myself. I question if what he's said is just a kind man trying to make me feel better. I'm sure you're tired of hearing this, and so am I. Why can't I accept what he says and be joyful?"

A stream of breath escaped Ally's lungs. "You've disliked yourself for a long time, Marcy, and it's hard to accept that you are loveable. You don't trust what you hear, but it's time you did."

"No one likes a pity-party. I know that. I hate it, but here I am falling into the party-pit."

Ally grinned. "A party-pit is a gaming table for gambling. I don't think you're a gambler, but maybe, to you, taking a chance with Grif is a gamble. Still I don't think so. He's rarely dated, and when he has been with a woman it's usually a long-time friend or a woman from church when he's working on a project."

"I'm a short time friend, so I guess I'm not part of the party-pit in any way." She shrugged. "I did see him with Iris, one of his long-time friends, but he explained that."

"Right. And can you count on your fingers how much time Grif has spent with you? Just teaching you about horseback riding took hours and hours. Then add on the other social events. Oh, Marcy, open your eyes and see that wonderful man for what he is. A gem in human form."

Her chest tightened. Ally hit the target. "He is wonderful. And he's put up with me and has tried to help me be who I want to be, not who he wants me to be."

"Then let him help you. You've made huge steps in opening up and learning new things. You are riding the horses now and—"

"Trotting. Not really out there galloping. I wish I could try that. It would make riding more fun for him."

"And for you. You can…with practice. Grif has the patience. Now all you need is the courage." Ally smiled.

Seeing her friend's confidence, Marcy's spirit brightened. "You're right. That's what I can do. I'll ask him if he wants to give it a try. I'm sure he will."

Ally gave her a thumb's up, and then eyed her watch. "He'll jump at the chance, Marcy. I know he will. And now look at the time. I'm going to be late getting back from lunch."

"Oops. Me too." They both scooted back their chairs and rose, carrying their trays to the dish conveyor belt and hurried into the hallway.

Ally gave her a wave, and she followed hoping that

no one noticed she'd returned late and without eating her meal. As she rushed back, she thought about ways she could show Grif that she had changed, and she wanted him to know what hadn't changed were ways in which she wanted to grow. The horseback riding seemed the simplest first step. Otherwise, her mind went blank.

What else could she do to prove her courage had grown as had her love for Grif. She'd always wanted to keep her feet on the ground, but she'd shown some improvement with horseback riding. Now she had to go a step further, but how or what?

Her mind was a blank.

♥

Grif leaned back against the stall frame, his mind jumping from image to image like a bucking stallion. Marcy had called, her voice giving her away. She'd been excited, and as always, he had no idea why. His understanding of women was lacking. Very lacking. And having fallen for someone like Marcy made it even worse. Sometimes he sensed she was talking in code. She had never learned to say what she means, but now that he knew her better, he had learned what had hindered her ability to communicate with him.

With what he'd learned about Marcy's father, he gave thanks that he would never meet the man. If he had, he feared he wouldn't have been able to hold back his frustration with a father who'd intimidated his daughter so badly. He prayed that one day Marcy could heal from her father's harsh and cruel attitude.

Yet her call today left him confused. Something had happened, but what? He'd have to wait to know, but that would be soon. She said she would drop by after work. He checked his watch, and his heart skipped. She would be there soon, and then he would know.

Pulling himself from thought, Grif finished his tasks with the horses and left the stable. Outside, he stood a moment, admiring the lowering sunshine washing across the mountains. Their colors changed along with the sun's glow—from a gold glow to deepening shadows. Sometimes, his spirit took on the same colors. Today he volleyed between a glow and shadow, trying to imagine what Marcy had in mind.

Instead of pacing outside, he headed for the house and stepped inside. He glanced around the kitchen with dinner on his mind. Should he try to come up with a meal or take Marcy out to dinner? But he had no answer until he better understood what caused the excitement in her voice. Or would he ever know? That was Marcy. She gave him hope, yet sometimes left him confused.

After perusing the refrigerator, the idea of cooking left him. They could go out or order something for delivery. He'd let Marcy decide.

Grif forced his mind on anything but Marcy's arrival, and when he heard a car door close, a shiver tingled down his back. Whether excitement or concern, When he heard her footsteps, he moved toward the door and opened it.

Marcy stopped and smiled. "You look surprised."

"Me? I'm not surprised, I knew you were coming, but curious, I guess."

"Curious? Why?"

He shook his head, startled that she would ask that question. He managed a chuckle rather than try to explain. "On the phone, you sounded as if you had some good news."

"Not news, really, but a proposition." She stepped further from the doorway and moved closer to him.

"A proposition? Now I'm even more curious." He reached out and caught her shoulder. "I'm curious about what you have on your mind? Does it involve dinner?"

She chuckled and shook her head. "That is the second thing on my mind." She shifted her arm around his back. "I don't really have a plan, Grif, but whatever we do, I want you to help me decide."

He still had no idea what she was talking about or what she wanted to decide. He kept his mouth closed, not wanting to push her. She'd been through enough. Taking it slow seemed the best decision for him. He just nodded with a smile. Marcy appeared satisfied.

"Would you like to go out for dinner, or I can order in if you prefer?" He studied her expression.

"Let's stay here, Grif. We can talk and not feel rushed."

He liked her choice, and after discussing what she might want for dinner, they settled on Ming House for Chinese. Grif brought up their menu on his cell phone and they made a list. "Do I have this right, Marcy. Won ton soup, veggie rolls, Moo Shu pork, almond chicken, and white rice."

"Is this a banquet?" Marcy grinned. "Or do you like leftovers?"

"I'm a leftover eater, but it gives us a nice variety, and don't forget, they'll give us a fortune cookie free. You can't resist that can you?"

Color rose on her cheeks. "I might enjoy seeing my fortune, Grif. I've often wondered what would happen to me."

"Good, then I'll order." She looked innocent with the slight blush on her cheeks, and he hoped that their talk could be constructive. He had so much to say, but tonight would be her time to open up. He clicked on the phone number, placed the order, and then gave Marcy a wink. "Do you want to talk now or after we eat. They said they'd deliver in about fifteen minutes."

"We can talk, but..." She glanced at her watch. "Sure, why not. What I have to say could be short...or maybe not, but we'll see."

Her response left him questioning again. Was this something simple to discuss or something serious? With Marcy lately, everything seemed a mystery. "I'll get us something to drink. What will you have? Water? Soft drink? Tea? Coffee?"

"For now, I'll have water."

He rose and left the room, his mind flipping from one idea to the next, as he put ice in a glass and filled it with water. He grabbed a soft drink for himself and returned to the living room. "Here you go."

She'd settled in a corner of the sofa, her knees drawn up beside her, and when he extended the glass, she clasped it. "Thanks." She took a sip and set it on the lamp table, and then patted the cushion next to her. "So..."

She appeared to study his face as if searching for something, and as curious as she apparently was, he studied hers.

Finally, she looked into his eyes. "Why are you smiling, Grif? Did I do something funny?" She shifted her hand to his cheek.

Grif covered her fingers with his palm. "No, you

did nothing funny or nothing at all but look at me with those beautiful eyes

"Beautiful? Me? Marcy, no one has ever said…"

"No, it's not you, Grif. It's your eyes that are beautiful. You're handsome."

His frown shifted to a grin. "Thank you, but I—"

"You can't admit it because you're a rugged rancher. Is that right?"

"Well…" He lowered his hand and chuckled. "I suppose no one has ever called me handsome."

"You are, Grif. You are handsome on the inside and the outside. You're one of the nicest people I know, and I've failed to let you know that, I guess. I should have…" She sought his gaze, realizing what she'd done. "I've been so focused on my shortcomings and lack of talents, that I never thought to tell you what I see when I look at you."

"If we're being honest, Marcy, to me you are beautiful in every way. I've learned to love your…, as you tend to call them, your shortcomings. That's what has made you 'you,' and the only reason I would love to see you forget some of them is that I want you to enjoy the fullness of your life and who you are. None of us are perfect, but we all have qualities that make us special and worthy."

Her pulse skipped. "Grif, this is what I want to talk to you about."

"None of us is perfect? Is that what you want to—"

"No, I want to tell you that I'm ready to seek that fullness of my life that you've talked about. I want to grow even more and be courageous and not fearful and holding myself back. I realize that I've lived my father's words without understanding how they affected me. I understand now."

Grif gasped her hands in his. "Do you, Marcy?" His serious expression morphed to a grin. "If you do, then you can grow and explore what life has to offer you. You already know how much I care about you, and I've wanted to see you live, unhampered by your father's horrible statement about a woman's place. He was wrong and you know that."

"I do. But now I really do. So...I'm ready to give up being a coward, but I need you to help me. I want to do some things that I've struggled with. I took small steps all my life. Today, I want to take bigger steps, and the first one is to ride Belle, but not just a trot."

"You want to canter?"

"Gallop." She nodded, determined to change her life from fear to adventure, like Ally.

"No galloping without learning to canter. Take it slow, and only if you're sure after you think about it, Marcy. You know Belle is a good horse. You've ridden her before, so you know how she responds to your directions."

"I signal her with my legs or the reins. I remember that."

"Then whenever you're ready, we'll do it. We'll begin trotting and then you can learn to canter. But only when you're ready. And later, you'll learn to gallop."

He held his breath, unsure of where the conversation was going. "What else do you have in mind to change?"

She shrugged. "I'm not sure, but I know I want to be braver."

"One step at a time. You can..."

"Let's go riding now, Grif. What do you think?"

He studied her from head to toe. "You're dressed right for riding, but we just ordered dinner." He grinned at her. "I'm guessing you had riding in mind when you came, didn't you?"

"No, not really. I wanted to tell you what I just said, but I never thought about riding until it made sense as we were talking."

"Good. That means it's something you planned inside. You really want to make some changes. I love hearing that, Marcy."

"Me, too."

"Let's enjoy dinner tonight, and we can ride tomorrow. I'll teach you everything I know and one day you'll be an excellent rider. How's that? And we can start tomorrow."

"Hmm?" She tilted her head upward as her mouth curved to a grin. "It's wonderful, Grif. Really wonderful. And you're right. Tonight, I'm starving."

♥

Grif checked his watch, his gaze shifting to the driveway and then back to his watch. Marcy sounded eager to ride yesterday and said she'd be there by noon, but noon had long since passed. His thoughts shifted from irritation to concern. What could have happened?

Their recent conversation left him with high hopes. Marcy had made great strides, letting go of her old fears, the influence of her father's unkind words, and gaining determination to grow. That's what he'd wanted to hear. Yet today, he waited and wondered.

Instead of wasting time, he opened the stable doors and guided Lady and Dusty to the corral. They needed his attention and love as much as anyone. His eyes still shifting to the driveway, he decided to give up and go indoors. He'd scrimped on breakfast and his growling stomach reminded him.

Inside his kitchen, he pulled out a hunk of cheese and opened a package of crackers. Not much, but something to stave off the grumbling inside him. At least that was better than the grumbling that filled his mind. He lowered his head, hearing again Marcy's enthusiasm about changing and growing. He'd never heard her sound so sincere about seeking a new life. Something may have happened, but nothing serious, he prayed.

Time ticked passed. He'd long given up on waiting and spent the morning and early afternoon exercising the horses and cleaning out the stalls. Inside, his thoughts hopped in one direction and then another. A phone call would have helped unless... he pushed away his imagination. Marcy worked at a hospital. Who could guess what might have stopped her from leaving and getting to a phone?

Instead of pacing, he got a grip on his wavering thoughts and sank into his recliner with a new copy of *Horse Illustrated* magazine. He eyed the articles and turned to one that caught his interest, but before he reached the end, a knock sounded on his door. He dropped the magazine and hurried toward the door.

Marcy eyed him with a guilty look written on her face. "I'm so sorry, Grif. I had to work this morning, but I had this afternoon off until one of the nurses couldn't make it in, and they asked me to stay until they had a replacement. I started to call, but—"

"I understand, Marcy." He managed a grin. "Those things happen."

"I wanted to call, but we were so busy and... Never

mind, we've lost enough time together. No more work talk."

He waved her toward the door. "It's mid-afternoon so we should go now before it's too late for today."

She understood and stepped toward the door, her nerves starting to rise but her determination grew even stronger. Grif followed her and then passed her as he hurried toward the barn. She didn't rush. Grif preferred to tack the horses, and she understood. One loose buckle could mean someone getting hurt. And today it could be her.

When she reached the stable, Grif had set the saddle pads and saddle on Russet and was attaching the cinch. When the cinch was tightened, he added the bridle. She loved seeing him tack the horse. "Sometime I'd like to learn how to get a horse ready for riding, Grif. I suppose it's not as easy as it looks."

He turned to her and grinned. "One step at a time, Marcy. You'll need to build some muscles to lift that saddle, but maybe one day you can do it."

She eyed the saddle and all the paraphernalia. "I think you're right. That saddle looks heavy."

"It's cumbersome, but if you want to learn, we'll give it a try one of the days. Right now, I think the task is riding."

She gave him a nod, irritated with herself for wanting to grow too fast. She knew better. "Right. I have to be less eager and more patient."

"You make me smile, Marcy."

Her grin grew. "And you make me very happy, Grif and that's why I smile."

Grif slipped his arm around her waist and drew her closer. "We were meant to be, Marcy. I'm certain. The

Bible says laughter is the best medicine and a smile is almost the same as laughter."

His comment touched her spirit and she couldn't help but laugh. "The sun's going to set before you get these horses ready."

He pressed his lips against her cheek and turned even faster to finish the tacking. She watched as he completed the job and checked all the connections and tilted his head toward the stable doorway. "Ready."

Her determination to grow in courage took a slight dip. Something about reality left her feeling different than making statements. Yes, she wanted to be courageous and stronger, but when the time came, some of her old doubts weighted her mind. She kept her mouth shut not wanting to let her fear win.

Outside, she stood next to Belle, stroking her mane and speaking to her in a soft voice. She did it for the horse and also for herself.

Grif stood back, as if waiting for her to mount Belle on her own. She knew how, but doing it was different. Hanging on to determination, she stepped closer, grasped the saddle's horn, slipped her left foot into the stirrup and swung her right leg over the saddle. Though Grif's voice was hidden beneath her hammering heart, the broad smile on his face said more than his words.

He mounted and walked Russet to her side. "Let's only trot across the field before speeding up. The horses will be more comfortable, and so will we."

Grif could jump on the saddle and begin galloping without a warm-up, but she understood he was protecting her. The sentiment sweetened his efforts to safeguard her. She flicked the rein and Belle trotted off following Grif on Russet. They rode side by side without conversation, but an occasional look showed his pleasure that she was beside him, and she felt the same in her heart.

Never in her life had she pictured herself with a man who cared about her. Being a wife and maybe a mother hadn't even been a dream. She didn't love herself, so how could a man love her? The thought snagged her mind, and she gazed across the meadow toward the Mund Mountains and focused on the beauty of creation and the ruffle of a breeze in her hair.

Russet's clomp drew nearer as Grif rode closer, leaning away from the saddle. "Ready? We're more than half way. Just start picking up speed a little at a time. You'll feel the gallop when it happens."

"She gave him a nod, never having experienced a gallop or how it differed from trotting. Instead of over thinking, she prepared herself as she pressed her knees into Belle's shoulders. The horse gained speed, and she hung on trying to remember the things Grif had told her. The one thing she needed now, she remembered. In a canter or gallop sit as if she planned to jump which he explained was slightly above the saddle.

She kept her weight on her feet tucked as far as she could into the stirrups. She inched herself above the saddle and hung on. The tenser she became the tighter she used her knees and the faster Belle went. When she glanced at Grif, he was trying to get her attention, telling her to slow down. She knew what to do but her knees stayed glued to Belle.

"Grif, I can't relax enough to loosen my grip." She hoped he heard her, but she decided he hadn't, until he lifted his reins and tightened them. Russet slowed, and she understood.

Marcy lessened the hold with her knees, grasped the reins and tightened them slowly. Belle caught on and eased the canter, or was it a gallop, to a trot. Her chest relaxed and air blasted from her lungs. She patted the mare and again drew back the reins. Belle came to a stop, and again she patted her. "Good girl, Belle."

Before she could dismount, Grif had hurried to her side. "Are you okay?"

"You answer that." She looked down from the saddle. "I'm still on the horse."

A grin relaxed his expression. "And thank the Lord for that, Marcy. I was worried that you would panic…but you didn't. I'm very proud of you."

"Thanks. I'm proud of myself. For a moment there, I was trying to figure out how to get off

the horse without stopping."

Grif's eyes widened, though in a second he grinned. "I hope you're kidding."

She smiled back. "Sort of. I knew better."

He reached up and helped her to the ground, leaving his arms around her waist as they stood beside Belle. Grif's thoughts were evident, and seeing his expression, Marcy's were too. She needed to go slower. She couldn't learn everything in a few hours. Next time, she would be more careful.

"Let's go inside for now. You can work on cantering tomorrow. If you're not tense, I am."

Marcy chuckled. "Sorry. I know it's not funny, but I will say it was an experience and, in the past, I would have said 'no more lessons for me.' But I hope you noticed that I didn't. I want to learn and do it right next time."

He gave her another squeeze and handed her the

reins. "Let's get the horses back to the stable. We need to give them water and then untack them. There's a whole routine to follow after riding, but I think you know most of it."

"I've seen you do it, Grif, but I want to learn how to do it myself, too."

"You will. Today you'll get your first lesson."

She playfully rolled her eyes, yet happy to find herself so eager to learn new things.

Grif moved ahead holding Russet's reins and walking him toward the stable, although Russet seemed to be guiding Grif. The horse knew where he was headed. She followed Grif's example and lead Belle in the same direction. Handling Belle seemed a breeze, and she looked forward to learning what needed to be done following riding.

♥

Marcy sank into one of Grif's easy chairs, happy to have untacked and groomed Belle. She'd seen Grif's pride that she'd caught on, and she loved feeling the same way. Too much of her life had been spent being ashamed of who she was.

"How about some food? You must be starving."

"I'm surprised I'm not." Marcy's lips curved to a grin. "I've learned that riding a horse takes all my concentration and food takes a back step."

"Still, we need to eat. I'll find something, I'm sure. You just sit there, and I'll be back."

Marcy leaned back in the chair and closed her eyes, but the sounds of him banging around in the kitchen kept her from falling asleep. She straightened in the chair and noticed a magazine he'd left on the lamp table. She leaned over and grasped it as she read the magazine title. *Horses*. She would expect him to learn everything he could about horses. She wanted to do the same. Scanning the index, an article on riding horses caught her interest, and she turned to the page and grinned when she noticed the diagrams and photos of people mounted on horses. She used it as a quiz for herself, but the test ended when Grif returned and stood in front of her.

"I made you a ham sandwich with cheddar cheese." He lowered the plate. "Is that okay?"

"It's one of my favorite sandwiches.

He breathed a sigh. I thought so…or I should say, I hoped so."

She tilted her head toward the magazine. "I thought I could learn something, and I did." She placed the magazine back where she'd found it and reached for the sandwich plate.

Hungrier than she thought, she bit into the toasted bread, pleased that he'd taken time to melt the cheese. "Delicious, Grif. Thanks."

"Glad you like it." He took another bite of his sandwich, and they both remained quiet as they finished the food.

"Hopefully that will hold us for a while." Grif rose and took her plate. "I'll get us something to drink. Coffee, tea, water?"

"Water's fine, Grif."

He vanished and she leaned back again, reviewing the mistakes she'd made on the horse, but also recalling the things she did right. Finding the positive things made her smile.

"What's funny?"

Grif's voice startled her. "Nothing. I was thinking

about what I did wrong today and what I did right. Finding the good things made me smile."

"They make me happy, too, Marcy. You said you wanted to learn and grow, and that smile lets me know that it's what you're doing."

He settled on the sofa and patted the cushion next to his. "Come over here."

Her heartbeat skipped, seeing the look on his face. She rose and sank beside him. "It's been a good day, even though I was late."

"But not too late to get a start."

"It's not, and now I have more riding experience, some right and some wrong."

"You'll learn, Marcy." His arm slipped behind her shoulders and he drew her closer. "Seeing you out there warmed my heart. I remember when we first met. I never thought you'd be on a horse, but here you are, and it makes me very happy."

"Me, too, Grif. You make me happy."

His eyes captured hers, and his free hand slipped to her cheek and eased her closer. His lips parted and she leaned in, already feeling breathless and eager to kiss his enticing lips.

When he eased back and studied her face, she melted with little control. How could one man cause her to feel as she did? His palm brushed her cheek again, and as he leaned toward her, the doorbell rang. Grif jerked back, surprise on his face. He gave her a shrug as he rose and hurried to the door.

Even with the interruption, she'd said all she needed to say, and getting it off her mind made her feel lighter and ready to broaden her steps.

She recognized Cade's voice at the door, but she

couldn't hear what they were saying. Their laughter followed the talk, and in a moment, Grif hurried into the room. "I can't believe what just happened. It was as if our voices floated outside."

"Huh?" She wrinkled her nose trying to make sense of Grif's comment.

"That was Cade. He said he and Ally were planning to go out riding and wondered if you and I would like to come along. His words, 'It's a beautiful day,' and it is."

"You and me?" She gaped at him, almost believing that her voice had ridden out on the wind. "Why did they include me?"

"Grif said they'd watched you trotting and figured they could take it slow so you could come too, but we can surprise them, if you really want to try a gallop."

She faltered before yanking up her courage. "Why not? That gives me motivation to do my best." But as the words left her, fear rifled through her. "If I can't, I can't."

"But you can." Grif drew her closer and gave her a hug. "I'm proud of you, Marcy. I really am."

Chapter 13

Grif tacked Lady and Cade helped saddle Biscuit, while Marcy and Ally sat on a hay bale near the stable doorway. Grif heard them chuckling and spotted a smile on Marcy's face as his spirit soared. He had longed for the day when Marcy gained confidence and knew she could learn new things. Her release from the chains that had bound her filled his heart. He needed nothing more.

Cade tightened the cinch on Biscuit first and led him to the stable doorway. He stopped a moment saying something to the women, and then continued outside. Grif hurried around to the right side of Lady and attached the cinch to the off billet, then returned to the left side and tightened the cinch with the latigo. He gave Lady a pat and guided her through the stable door to join Biscuit.

Marcy looked at him, her eyes questioning, and he eased closer to her. "Are you okay? We can say no."

"I'm fine, Grif. Just feeling my bravery is slipping a bit, but—"

"Marcy, we should all question ourselves. If you're not comfortable or aren't ready for cantering, then don't. You can trot. I know you're comfortable with the slower pace, and I'll stay behind with you."

Her shoulders lifted with the release of a sigh. "No, I'm not a baby. I can keep up…I hope."

"Promise to give me a signal if you want to slow down or stop. I'll handle it." He searched her face looking for a reaction, but she remained stoic.

"I'm okay. Really, I am. I want to be able to do this. And I will."

This time he released a lengthy breath, weighing her words before he finally gave in. "Great. Then, let's mount."

Ally and Cade had already settled on their horses, but Grif waited beside Biscuit to make sure Marcy mounted without a problem, and she did. He loved seeing her slip her left foot into the stirrup and swing her right leg over the saddle. His chest puffed with pride, and when she looked his way, he gave her a thumbs up and mounted.

The horses were steered toward the meadow, and as he expected, Ally and Cade went on ahead. He held back on purpose, wanting Marcy to know he wasn't anxious to canter along with them. But his attempt failed his purpose. As she often did, Marcy wanted to be part of the group. She refused to listen to any concerns she had, too determined to stay with the others.

He wanted to trust her. He cared about her more than he could say, and enjoying her confidence and new adventurous actions, he cantered beside her, almost keeping up with the other two. When he saw Cade turn to look for them, he shifted the reins to encourage Biscuit to speed up, and the horse did.

Irritated with himself, he shifted his legs and the

reins to slow again. He didn't want Marcy to feel left out. That could be a setback. Once he slowed, Marcy appeared at his side, gave him a grin, and moved forward on the saddle, letting Lady know to pick up speed. She surprised him, and he hurried ahead too, just in case.

In case? Why did that thought enter his mind? Marcy looked in control and happy, and his concern dwindled as he checked on Ally and Cade. When he looked back, he noticed that Marcy seemed to have shifted her weight to the right on the saddle. His worry rose and though he called her name, she ignored him.

His pulse picked up, positive that something had happened, the saddle appeared to be sliding and Marcy rode with it. He yelled her name again, and when she turned, his heart rose to his throat when he realized the saddle had slid to the right and Marcy with it, somehow hanging on. He picked up pace and caught Lady's reins, trying to stop her, yet fearing that if he slowed her too fast, Marcy could fall to the ground and in Lady's confusion, the mare could trot on her.

Cade and Ally had finally noticed, since he saw them coming back, Grif jumped down from the stallion and raced to Lady's side. Marcy had somehow clung to the saddle, but her head hung too close to the ground. One rock or rise in the earth could injure her. He spoke the horse's name and slowed her to a stop.

When he did, Grif reached down and held Marcy in his arms, while Cade removed her boots from the stirrups. Together they eased her to the ground without harm. Grif's heart raced, pounding with such force his chest hurt. "Lord, thank you." He knelt in the meadow grass, drawing Marcy closer against his chest. "Are you hurt, Marcy?"

"I don't think so." A quiver sounded in her voice.

Ally had begun to search her arms and legs for scratches or wounds while Grif studied the saddle.

"I don't know what happened, Marcy. Please forgive me. I saddled Lady as I always do so I don't understand why the saddle slipped."

Cade shifted closer to the saddle, giving Lady friendly pats while he eyed the cinch and billet and frowned before turning to Grif. "The only thing I can think of is that Marcy tended to lean to the right. A saddle can slip if it's not cinched tight enough. That's rare, but it could happen."

Grif eyed the saddle and checked the cinch. "I double checked the cinch. I'm certain it was tight enough. Too tight isn't good for Lady, so I—"

"Don't blame yourself, Grif. Marcy's an inexperienced rider and if she leaned too far right, that can happen. You know that as well as I do."

Grif's irritation rose, and he tried to give Cade a look to stop blaming Marcy. She'd never get back on a horse if she believed she was the blame.

Cade gave a one-shoulder shrug and became silent, while Grif wished the confrontation hadn't occurred. Yes, he could be at fault and it could have been Marcy, but he didn't want to dwell on blame. He only wanted to thank the Lord for her safety.

He dropped the subject and eased Marcy up from the ground, his arm baring her weight. "Do you feel okay?"

He nodded. "I'm fine, Grif. Really, and Cade might be right. I could have easily leaned to the right. I am a new rider, and I'm sure I'll make a few mistakes until

I'm more seasoned as a horseman...or horsewoman." She flashed him a grin.

Seasoned? Grif never thought he'd hear those words, nor had he expected to see her grin. He'd suspected that Marcy would say never again. She would have said it months ago, but her comment left him hopeful. People could transform, and Marcy had shown a transformation in many ways. He needed to prove his faith in her.

He grasped Lady's reins. "I'd better get her back to the stable, and—"

"Why?" Marcy's voice cut through his plan. "How can we ride if I don't have a horse? You can't blame Lady, Grif. You know it was my doing. I'd like to get back on and ride. You know what they say, and I read this in your horse magazine. 'If you fall off a horse get right back on, and if you fall seven times, get back on the eighth time.'"

Grif's eyes widened so much he sensed his brows had reached his hairline. "You read that in my magazine?"

"I did. I wanted to learn more about riding, and I did learn. I'm perfectly fine. No scratches, no broken bones. Nothing but wanting to get back on."

Grif drew her into his arms, and despite their audience, he kissed her with a lingering kiss that took his breath away. "Marcy, you are amazing."

Her rosy lips turned to a grin. "I am, and I love it. No more fear. No more guilt. No more self-loathing."

Cade and Ally broke into applause before Ally drew closer. "Marcy, I've watched you change, and I'm so proud of you. We all are. You've made more progress than I have in a lifetime."

Marcy opened her arms and gave Ally a hug. "Thank you. That means the world to me." She turned to Grif. "Grif has been patient as a saint, and I'm so happy that he stuck with me since the change not only means the world to me, but I know it means the world to him.

Although Grif nodded, he took Marcy's hands and drew her to him. "Marcy, it's you that means the world to me. I don't think I can live without you."

Her head snapped back, and in silence, she studied his face. "You're kidding, right?"

"Not one word is a joke. I love you, Marcy. To me, this is no longer a friendship. It's so much deeper than that. You are my world."

"I'm your..." Her jaw dropped as she turned to Ally and Grif. "Did you hear what he said?"

They both grinned. "We'd have to be deaf not to have heard him, Marcy." Ally stepped toward her. "I knew this day would come. Cade and I both did. We've been waiting to hear you admit how much Marcy means to you."

Grif shook his head. "I should have planned this day a little different. Some place special." As the words flew from him, a plan rose in his mind. "How about dinner? I owe you all a dinner for being such good friends and—"

"You owe us nothing. We were here, and glad we could help you."

Grif didn't let Cade's comment stop him. "How about tonight? Can you make it. It's my treat, and it will be special."

Cade gave Ally a playful poke in the side. "We're on. When I can get a special dinner from you, my friend, I'll be there."

"Good." He nestled closer to Marcy. "Can we finish the horseback ride tomorrow? We need to get dressed for dinner."

She wrapped her arms around his waist, her eyes sparking with happiness. "Absolutely. I have a very nice dress I wore at a wedding not too long ago, and I'll wear that." She gave Ally a wink.

Grif eyed his watch. "Let's meet at seven. I'll make reservations somewhere if I can and let you know."

♥

Elote didn't offer reservations. They would have to wait on the large porch until seating was available, so he thought of another place he liked on the Hillside. The Hudson was a fine restaurant on an upper level with lovely views of the red rocks and rolling mountains.

Though he'd confessed his feelings, the admission surprised him. He'd planned to talk to Marcy in private, a time to tell her how he felt and that he wanted her as his wife and mother of their children.

He'd never learned how to be romantic, but he hoped, despite his bold admission that Marcy felt the same. She'd done much to please him. She'd stepped out of her comfort zone and ended up enjoying many new experiences. She'd gotten braver and braver, and it touched his heart.

When he checked his watch, he faltered, unaware that time had flown and he needed to get dressed. He studied his closet and noticed a huge lack in his clothing. He didn't have a real suit for a special occasion, except for his gray wedding and funeral suit, and that was too much for a dinner—even a special one.

Searching further, he found a sort of Western sport jacket that worked well with a pair of trousers he owned, and though he dug around for a tie, he gave up, hoping a dress shirt open at the collar would still look fine for the evening. He tucked the small velvet box into his jacket pocket while his pulse skipped beats. Tonight, would be an experience he never anticipated. Never.

When he climbed into his SUV, his mind slipped back to Marcy's horrifying slip from the saddle. He'd gone over and over the details of tacking Lady. He'd tightened the cinch, he'd checked the billets, the saddle blanket was the proper size and placed in the right spot under the saddle, so what went wrong? The more he thought, he realized that he may have been careless with girth. If the saddle hadn't been centered and tight enough, Marcy's inexperience—maybe leaning to the right—could have caused her to slip sideways. He thanked the Lord more than once for her safety.

His mind full, he faltered when he realized he'd reached Marcy's home. He pulled into the driveway and stepped from the car. He'd called Cade and Ally who lived in Sedona, and they agreed to meet them at the Hudson. Grif couldn't wait to enjoy this special, and romantic night with friends and with the woman he longed to be with for a lifetime.

As he reached her door, it opened, and Marcy stood in the opening dressed in the pretty dress she'd worn for Cade and Ally's wedding. His breath caught in his throat as he pictured waking with her each morning, her hair tousled, yet a smile on her lips. "You look gorgeous, Marcy."

She pushed the door open wider and stepped back.

"I'm ready, but come in. I want to take a sweater or something in case it's cool later on."

He followed her inside feeling the box in his pocket, considering when he should give it to her, but he stopped himself from being tempted to do it now, since Cade and Ally wanted to be part of the special day in their lives.

Marcy returned in a moment, and he held her hand as they walked to the SUV. He opened the door and she settled onto the seat while his excitement grew. He rounded the vehicle and dropped in beside her. "Ally and Cade are meeting us there."

She eyed him a moment and smiled. "Where?"

"You'll see when we get there."

She gave her head a playful shake and leaned back.

With no more words, he backed out of the driveway and headed down Cornville Road to 89A and made a right toward West Sedona. He struggled with conversation since all he could think about was the ring box in his pocket and the words he wanted to say when they arrived.

They pulled up the hill and headed for the back of the building. As he parked, Cade and Ally stepped from their car close by. Ally beckoned Marcy to her side, and Grif took the chance to talk with Cade.

"Thanks for coming with us, Cade. I almost blew it, but it worked out and I'm glad. I wanted us to have a romantic dinner and to get down on my knees."

Cade slapped Grif on the back. "You did get on your knees, Pal. You just missed the dinner."

They chuckled, reliving Grif kneeling on the ground holding Marcy in his arms while she remained hanging from the horse.

They were still laughing when Marcy and Ally arrived at their side, and they both gave them a strange look. Ally's grin turned to a frown. "What's so funny?"

"Nothing." Cade arched a brow, probably hoping Ally wouldn't continue to question him.

She shrugged and followed Cade to the Hudson's entrance while Grif linked his arm to Marcy's and walked behind them.

Inside, Grif moved forward and spoke to the host who gathered menus and handed them to a waiter standing nearby. He led them to a table along the windows where the lowering sun colored the red rocks in shades of coral, pink and gold.

After the waiter left, they all studied the menu, except Grif whose heart hammered against his chest until he couldn't breathe.

Marcy turned to him. "Don't tell me you aren't hungry, Grif."

"No, I'm just thinking about what I want. I looked at the menu online."

Her brow wrinkled and she squinted at him. "You did what? You don't plan ahead like that."

He straightened his back, hoping he could sound amused. "I do sometimes, Marcy. You don't know all my secrets yet."

"Ah, you have secrets." She grinned and gave him a teasing pat.

"Not really. I do like to look when it's a place I don't go often." He opened the menu hoping he'd stop her probing questions.

It worked, Marcy opened her menu too. He forced himself to view the choices before gazing at Marcy. "I think I'll have the Salmon and how about the bruschetta for an appetizer?"

"Sounds good." She gave him a nod.

Ally closed the menu. "The baby-back ribs sounds great." She turned to Marcy. "Are you going to eat?"

Marcy shook her head. "Me? No." Then she grinned. "I can't decide between two entrees, but I think I'll go for the Parmesan chicken. I know I love that."

"Okay, and drinks?" Grif held up the menu and listed off their choices. Most settled for water and later coffee. "You are all too easy. Enjoy the day. Have something special."

Cade reached across the table and gave Grif's shoulder a shake. "This evening is special enough. I'll stick with coffee."

Once the order was placed, they settled back sipping water, except for Ally's iced tea.

Grif took a deep breath and straightened in the chair. "You all know this is a special night, I hope a romantic night, and I'm sure I'm not fooling anyone. I've already told you how I feel, Marcy. I've watched both of us grow into two people who need each other. I was a loner for many years. Cade, you know that, and I never thought I would change, but I have."

Marcy eyed him her brow furrowed. "You've changed a little but not much, Grif."

"But I have Marcy. I never saw myself as a husband or father or a man who courted a woman. It never entered my mind."

She drew back as her eyes widened. "You've told me I changed, Grif, and I admit that I have. I feared everything, but you opened windows and doors for me, and I'm very grateful. Life is much more meaningful and fun and all because of you."

"And you've helped me, Marcy. Don't deny it."

She studied him a moment and nodded. "Yes, I see a difference."

"And the biggest difference is that I told you how I feel about you. I can't imagine life without you, Marcy. Since I met you, I felt lost and empty without you. Do you understand?"

She sat in silence, her eyes searching his face. "Yes, and I understand too well, because I feel the same."

"Then, let's do something about it." He pulled himself up from the chair and went to her side, bending his knees to the floor. "Marcy, I not only care about you. I love you. I've never thought of marriage, but since meeting you that's all that's been on my mind." He reached into his pocket and pulled out the velvet box and opened the lid.

Marcy's eyes widened while tears blurred her eyes. "Grif, it's beautiful. I've never seen a ring this lovely, and the beautiful diamonds—" She faltered, brushing tears from her eyes.

"Marcy, will you be my wife and the mother to my children? Will you accept this ring as a promise that I will love you always and be the best husband I can be?"

Ally's faint sob caught everyone off guard, and when they turned back to Marcy, tears ran down her cheeks. "Grif, I never saw myself as a wife or mother. Never. I had no confidence that I could make anyone happy or raise children to feel loved and have confidence."

Grif's eyes glazed as he listened, praying she wouldn't say no. He pressed his left hand to his heart. "Marcy no one in the world deserves to be loved and desired any more than you. I've seen you with Chloe and Jolie. You made my heart sing. You were kind, fun, tender, creative and everything a child would want. You will be an amazing mother."

"But—"

"No 'but', Marcy." Ally grasped her hand. "I saw you with those girls and you were amazing. I've never lied to you, and I never will. Believe me and say yes. Grif and I have been waiting for this to happen for a long time."

Marcy's head lowered. She remained silent a moment, and then raised her eyes to Grif's. "I love you too, Grif." Her gaze shifted back to the ring. "You've surprised me. The ring is beautiful. Perfect."

He lifted it from the velvet bed and grasped her hand and slipped the ring on her finger. "Marcy, will you marry me?"

As tears dripped down her cheeks, a smile brightened her face. "Yes. Yes. Yes, Grif. I will marry you. I'll be your wife and with God's blessing, the mother to our children."

He drew her from the chair, wrapped her in his arms and kissed her with the deepest love he'd felt for any woman. Ally and Cade applauded and stepped forward, wrapping their arms around them and hugging them as they whispered blessings and expressed their happiness. Nothing could have been more perfect than sharing the special day with their friends.

As the waiter approached and hesitated, they burst into laughter and settled into their seats, trying to contain themselves while the man placed their meals on the table. When he left, Ally spoke first, surprising Grif. "When's the wedding, Grif? Soon?"

His jaws dropped, not sure how Marcy would respond. "What do you say, Marcy?" His own answer reverberated in his head. Soon. Soon.

Marcy paused a moment before lifting her gaze to his. "Whenever you're ready, Grif." She glanced at Ally and Cade. "How about tomorrow?"

Grif's heart danced. "Anything for you, Marcy. Soon. Very soon."

Her 'very soon' rang through his body, and he kept Marcy's hand in his until he had to let go to allow her to eat. Though he'd always love the Sedona sunrise, tonight he would never forget the Sedona Sunset they witnessed through the wide panorama of windows. Colors of pink, lavender and pastel blue adorned the sky and rested on the shadowy red rocks, hidden by the sinking sun.

The colors merged into his tender image of Marcy, reflecting her softness, beauty, and expectation that sunsets bring to each new day in his life, another day, a gift of time to share with her wrapped in the sweetness of sunrises and sunsets.

Chapter 14

With Marcy's playful response to his proposal, tomorrow sounded better and better to Grif. They hadn't talked details yet, but he couldn't stop coming up with ideas so they would be ready and soon. He'd thought about a barn wedding which had worked well for Ally and Cade. Yet something caused him to want more for Marcy. She'd spent her life thinking she was unworthy, and though she had grown in many ways, he wanted her wedding to be a beautiful memory she would never forget. The more he thought about it, the more confused he became. What did he know about planning a wedding?

The one person who could help him came to his mind and gave him confidence. Ally knew Marcy well, and she would want the best for her too. He checked with Cade and learned that Ally had gone shopping but would be home soon. He said he'd have her call.

Though counting on Ally, Grif took in a lengthy breath and sank into his favorite chair. What would work and how could he surprise Marcy with an amazing wedding without her knowing every detail? He couldn't. Or could he? He leaned back, laughing at himself for even thinking he could surprise Marcy with their wedding location.

Maybe Ally had already discussed the wedding with Marcy, and if they had, Ally would know what Marcy had in mind, but before he spoke with Ally, he decided to check around on his own.

He opened the latest newspaper and scanned the wedding venue ads. The one that struck him the most was Tlaquepaque. Driving from the Village of Oak Creek, they passed the outdoor market with its large fountains, cobblestone streets, artwork and even a chapel amid the fancy stores and galleries within the stucco walls and wrought iron gates. The wedding could be as unique as Marcy.

While images of the wedding rolled through his mind, his phone rang, and he knew before answering, the caller would be Ally. When he looked, he was right. "Hi, and thanks for calling Ally. He explained the reason for his call while she dropped in comments, the main one being Marcy should plan her wedding. Though he stiffened with the comment, she'd spoken the truth.

"I know Marcy will want to be part of the plan, Ally, but I wanted to give the location some thought. I know you and Cade had the barn wedding, and for you, that was perfect. You did a great job making the setting perfect, but Marcy has been without for so long, and I want to give thought to something really special. As special as she is to me."

"I understand, Grif. I'm trying to view this through Marcy's eyes, and I would want to have input into my wedding, and I'm sure she will too."

"What if I offer some suggestions and see what she wants to consider?"

Silence struck him for a moment until Ally cleared her throat. "If you put it that way, it makes sense, Grif. I don't want to discourage you. I only thought that most women want to be included in the planning."

"And Marcy will, Ally." He bit his lip, hoping he wasn't sorry for what he was going to say next. "For example, we could have a home wedding, not the barn but the house. I know Marcy has only a little family and I have none."

"But you have friends, and Marcy has them too."

Friends. He drew up his shoulders. "We haven't talked about a big or small wedding yet. I'm not sure what Marcy wants, but for either one, I'm thinking about location of the wedding." His idea of Tlaquepaque hung in his head like a neon sign. "I know there are some outdoor locations. I ran across a wedding being set up at Watson Lake, for example. They set up tents that look out over the rugged embankment."

Ally remained quiet, and he assumed she didn't like the idea. Neither did he. "But I want more for Marcy. What about Tlaquepaque?"

Ally's gasped rattled through the phone. "That's a gorgeous place, Grif, but that would be very expensive, and I know that—"

"You know what, Ally? Marcy's worth it. Money is important to have a good life, but Marcy is far more important to me. I can afford to plan a wedding there…that is if Marcy likes the idea. Have you ever looked at the grounds as a wedding location? They have a chapel. They have plenty of space outside for a wedding dinner. They have musicians available. They have special features—"

"That cost thousands of dollars, Grif. Marcy is a saver. She's not one to spend money on herself, and—"

"And that's my point. Marcy deserves, for once in her life, to have something very special to prove how worthy she. I love her with all my heart. I'm not a rich man, but I'm not poor either. I want to have our wedding be a lasting memory of what true love means."

Though he ran out of breath, Ally, too, remained silent. "I'm not trying to be a wastrel, but I want one time in Marcy's life, to give her a gift that lets her know how much she is loved."

"Grif, I understand, and yes, you are right. I'm looking at this from dollars and cents. You're looking at it with love and sense. Marcy will be thrilled beyond words."

"Thanks. I'll suggest choices so she's part of the planning, but I'm not talking money to her. I'm talking wedding day with the woman I love."

"And you both deserve that wonderful day, Grif, without me or anyone dampening yours spirit. I'm sorry. You're doing something beautiful. Something precious. I am thrilled to be part of the wedding and part of your lives. Thank you for being my friend."

"No need to thank me, Ally. You've been a dear friend to Marcy, and I should thank you. Not everyone has a good friend who really cares, and Marcy has that kind of friendship with you. So now that we've talked it over, I hope you can support me in this. I'm anxious to talk with Marcy, and I hope she's willing to be treated like a queen."

"Grif, I'll be there to support you, and I believe that Marcy loves you enough to agree with you. If not, I'm there. You both mean the world to me."

"Thanks so much, Ally. You and Cade have been good friends, and I'm confident that you'll stick by us. Now I'm praying that Marcy supports my idea for the wedding."

♥

Marcy settled in the bride's room, away from being seen by Grif. She'd been startled by his thoughts on the wedding, so much more elegant and expensive than she would have ever conceived, but once she visited the lovely chapel and the beautiful outdoor venue for their wedding dinner, her heart nearly burst. Grif's kindness seemed to grow, the more time she spent with him. She couldn't imagine a lifetime of being loved and cared for the way Grif had already shown.

She worked hard to forget her horrible past, and Grif had become her number one supporter of living now and not in the past. He knew her so well and put up with her difficulties she'd dragged along with her, but more and more, those fears and negative attitudes had faded and with his support and love, she'd sprouted like a blossom that had once been a weed.

She jumped when the door opened, but calmed as soon as Ally entered the room. She pointed to her watch. "It's almost time, Marcy." Ally stepped closer and opened her arms, wrapping her in an embrace. Lacy is pacing in front of the chapel. She's so excited that you asked her to be her matron of honor. She told me about her wedding, but said how beautiful yours was going to be."

"I feared you'd be sad that I didn't ask you, Ally, but—"

"Sad? Never. Marcy, I'm rejoicing with you that you found a sister after all those years. I would have been upset if you had asked me instead of Lacy. I'm here for you and I'll guide your guests to the reception area, which is so close, but I'll be there for you while you're having photos taken and signing the wedding papers."

"Wedding papers?" She studied Ally's face, having no idea what she was talking about.

"After the wedding, you need to sign the marriage certificate, as do the witnesses. It only takes a few minutes, but I'll be available to guide your guests to the reception as I said."

"You know more than I do, Ally." Her mind reeled with so many details to getting married. She had no idea and was pleased that others knew so she could take care of things.

Ally only laughed. "You look beautiful, Marcy. I thought you were making a mistake when you wanted a dress that was an off-white, but now that I see it on you, it's egg-shell colored and looks so beautiful with your autumn colored flowers. You made a good decision."

"Thanks, Ally. I had lots of worries as you can imagine. With the reception being outside, I fear we would have rain or cold weather, and here it is a glorious warm day with no hint of rain."

"You see. You just have to trust."

Marcy gave a quick nod, too aware of how little she trusted before she met Grif. He had helped her in so many ways, and having faith and trusting was one thing she'd learned from him.

A knock sounded on the door before it slipped open. Lacy peeked inside. "It's time. Everyone's in the chapel, and now it's Grif who's pacing."

They both chuckled as Ally handed Marcy her

bouquet and straightened her short veil while Lacy hurried out the door with the boutonnières for Grif and Cade, the best man.

Marcy stood a moment, her heart skipping, as happiness washed over her. "I never thought I would be a wife, Ally. For so long, I didn't think I was worthy, and I thank the Lord that my life has improved beyond my imagination. Grif has given me a new view of life, and you and Cade have also been part of that. I feel so blessed, and yes, my pulse is hammering, but only because I have never been happier."

"Then let's get moving, my dear friend, before Grif thinks you're a runaway bride."

Marcy grinned. "I suppose you're right."

Ally held open the door as Marcy swept through the opening, her gown flaring around her ankles, while her joy burst from her heart as she made her way to the white washed Chapel and the Spanish-style arched doorway, adorned with flowers. She paused, her gaze searching Ally's.

"They're in front, Marcy—Grif and Cade—and they're waiting."

A violinist began to play, signaling it was time for Marcy to begin her walk down the aisle. Her heels clicked on tile floor and her pulse ticked as she passed the leather seated-bench, each seat back adorned with flowers along the aisle. The details overwhelmed her, and again, she gave thanks that she'd found an amazing man like Grif.

Ahead she saw him smiling at her. She smiled back, forgetting about those who were seated, with her eyes only on Grif, handsome in his dark suit and tie. She longed to run into his arms, but she managed to monitor her steps.

When she reached Grif, he took her arm and drew her beside him, a faint ripple of nerves evident in his touch, and probably matching hers. They faced the minister, following his directions, the vows, the rings, the words of love, but what touched her most was the words, "I now pronounce you man and wife. You may kiss the bride."

Grif's eyes sparkled as he gazed at her lips. He leaned closer, his lips touching hers while her heart danced as it never had done before. Married. Husband and wife. A concept she'd never dreamed of, and yet today the gift became a reality. She had been blessed beyond her imagination, and she prayed that Grif felt the same, and when she looked at him, she had no doubt.

They turned to face their family and friends who rose, with smiles filling their faces. Seeing their joy filled her with assurance and happiness. Women should be heard and seen, especially by the man who loved them. Since their meeting, Grif had opened his heart and his life to her, and nothing could fill her or complete her more than the rancher who loved her.

The Beginning

About Gail

Best-selling and award-winning novelist, Gail Gaymer Martin is the author of contemporary romance and romantic suspense with 86 published novels and over four million books sold. Her novels have won numerous national awards, including: the ACFW Carol Award, RT Reviewer's Choice Award and Booksellers Best. Gail is the author of Writer Digest's *Writing the Christian Romance.* She is a founder of American Christian Fiction Writers and a member of Advanced Speakers and Writers. Gail is a keynote speaker at churches, civic and business organizations and a workshop presenter at conferences across the U.S. She lives with husband Bob in Sedona, AZ. Contact her by mail at: PO Box 20054, Sedona, AZ 86341 or on her website or social media.

Website:www.gailgaymermartin.com
Facebook:www.facebook.com/gail.g.martin.3
Twitter:http://twitter.com/GailGMartin
GoodReads: http://bit.ly/1e8Gt6D
LinkedIn: www.linkedin.com/in/gailgaymermartin

Recipe - I enjoy sharing a recipe from my novel. Though the meal is not in this book, I talked about Mexican food, so I want to share one of my favorite Mexican style breakfasts.

Breakfast or Lunch Quesadilla

Pkg of six inch flour tortillas
Shredded cheese of your choice - cheddar, Mexican blend, etc.
Diced slice of onion
Diced tomato (cherry or plum)
2 slices fried bacon (for each person)**

Cover half the tortilla with cheese
Add diced onion and tomato (about a tbsp of each)
Add meat bacon or another choice (see below)
Option: add guacamole or sliced avocado
Fold the unused half over the half with cheese and ingredients
Place in a fry pan or griddle on medium heat until cheese melts
Turn over to other side until the cheese melts

**Meat choices: fried bacon, diced ham, diced cooked chicken

Enjoy for breakfast or lunch.

Gail's Books from Winged Publication

Novels - *Reissues*
Dreaming of Castles 2014
Out On A Limb 2016
Over Her Head 2017
Love Comes To Butterfly Tree Inn 2017
A Love Unforeseen 2017
Loving Treasures
Loving Hearts
Loving Ways
Loving Care
Loving Promises
Loving Kisses
Loving Arms
Teacher's Pet (Former: Dad in Training)

Novels - New
Treasures Of Her Heart 2014
Romance By Design 2015
Mackinac Island Christmas 2017
Love in the Air 2018

Novellas   Reissues
An Open Door
Apples Of His Eye
Better To See You
Once A Stranger
Then Came Darkness
To Keep Me Warm
True Riches
Yuletide Treasures

Novellas - New
Lattes and Love Songs 2015

Apple Blossom Daze 2016
A Trip To Remember 2016
A Tucumcari Christmas 2016
Poppy Fields and You, 2017
Love Comes to Butterfly Tree Inn 2017
Tumbling Into Love 2017
Lost In Red Rock Country 2017
Autumn's Fresh Beginnings 2017

Collections

Christmas Potpourri
Forget Me Not Romances #1
Forget Me Not Romances #2
Love Blooms In The Here & Now
Mocha Marriage
Romance Across the Globe
Romance On The Run
Seven Mysterious Ladies
With This Ring
A Kiss is Still a Kiss
Get Your Kiss On Route 66
Valentine Matchmakers
All Mixed Up
Love In Danger
California
Second Change At Love
When Love Calls
The Hope of Christmas
Happily Ever After
Romancing The Wild
Returning Home
Coming Home Again
Songs of the Heart
Fall N' For You
Stranded

SEDONA SUNSET